Lawyers Are a
Dime a Dozen . . . .

Lawyers Are a Dime a Dozen . . . .

(IT'S CHIMPANZEES THAT ARE HARD TO GET!)

William B. Wolf, Jr.

Copyright © 1999 by William B. Wolf, Jr.

Library of Congress Number: 99-91292
ISBN #:   Hardcover   0-7388-0742-7
                Softcover   0-7388-0743-5

Author's Note: These tales are factually accurate in every respect save one; I have occasionally changed a name to protect the guilty.

This book was printed in the United States of America.

To order additional copies of this book, contact:
Xlibris Corporation
1-888-7-XLIBRIS
www.Xlibris.com
Orders@Xlibris.com

CONTENTS

With profound appreciation,
I dedicate this book to the lawyers in the family,
to wit, my beloved daughter, Professor (of Law) Susan M. Wolf, JD,
my late father, William B. Wolf, Sr., LLB,
and my late grandfathers,
Alexander Wolf, LLB, LLM, and
Samuel Bernard Pack, LLB, LLM.

"LAWYERS ARE A DIME A DOZEN . . . ."

Before my friend Jack went off to jail, in spite of the best efforts of Edward Bennett Williams and associates—Jack's crime boiled down to overenthusiasm, manifested by his sale of an unconscionably priced TV "system" to an unlettered black lady who happened to be blind, which an unsympathetic Federal jury construed to constitute "fraud by mail and wire"—he had greatly enriched my experience in the practice of law.

Little suspecting that Jack would one day make chimpanzees the focus of my law practice, I early classified Jack's approach to life as similar to that of the famous golfing gorilla in the old joke. You remember the joke: A fellow secretly trains his pet gorilla to hit a golf ball, takes him to the links to join the fellow's regular foursome, tees up the gorilla's drive, and basks in the awe of his companions as the gorilla drives the ball 400 yards onto the green. When the human foursome finally reaches the green, the fellow putts, then hands the gorilla his putter. The gorilla watches the rest of the foursome putt; when his turn comes, he hunches over the ball, addresses the putt, pulls the putter back, and hits the ball—400 yards. Well, that was Jack.

Jack launched my law practice. I had passed the bar examination and was awaiting the ceremonial induction when Jack walked into my cubbyhole of an office and announced that his mother was stealing him blind (then merely a figure of speech). Steered by my employer, I rooted around the local Probate office and excitedly found that his mother was indeed stealing him blind. Jack's father, who knew his Jack but not his wife, had died leaving a lot of money in trust for Jack, naming Jack's mother as the testamentary trustee. Jack's mother, who had very expensive tastes, proceeded to indulge said tastes to the fullest, which she did by treating the trust assets as her very own.

Surfacing once I was inducted into the bar, I was able to persuade Jack's mother's lawyer that his client would be well advised to come up with a pile of money and terminate Jack's interest in the trust with a cash settlement. With payment imminent, I took a leaf from Jack's father's book and (I thought) convinced Jack that the money should be placed in a bank-administered trust for the benefit of Jack and his wife.

On the appointed day, Jack's mother's lawyer came to my office with a certified check drawn to the order of my law firm and mutual releases pre-signed by Jack's mother. I took the releases into the conference room wherein sat Jack and his wife; Jack signed. I returned to my office, traded the releases for the check, and escorted Jack's mother's lawyer to the elevator. Then I went back to the conference room, handed Jack the indenture of trust I had drafted for him, and asked him to sign it and then come into my office, where I would be preparing checks to fund the new trust.

"No," said Jack.

"No, what?" I asked.

"No trust," Jack said. "I want the money."

I looked at Jack's wife. She shrugged her shoulders; I gave Jack a check for a lot of money. Over the next twelve months Jack bought—and sold, always at a loss—an even dozen of the best looking automobiles I had ever seen. Monthly, he would drive by my house in the new car; he appeared to have some notion that I was entitled to see his application of funds. They were all gone within a year.

Jack didn't really care; he could always make enough money as a salesman to pay the rent, put food on the table, and gas up whatever he was driving. But Jack had an entrepreneurial streak, as I found out one day when he ambled into my office (he never called first, having a pathological aversion to telephones) and announced, "I've just bought a pet shop; draw the papers." I sat him down and gave him the young lawyer's learned lecture re the Bulk Sales Act, the advisability of incorporation, the choice of jurisdictions, the beauties and traps of Subchapter S of the Internal Revenue Code, and my need for client instruction. He heard me out impassively; then he stood up, reached into his hip pocket, pulled out an enormous roll of bills, and peeled off part of the roll.

"Sounds like $3,000 worth of work," he said, dropping thirty $100's on my desk. "Take care of it." I took care of it.

A month or so later, the telephone rang one morning; it was Jack. His use of the telephone was startling; so was his message. "Read this turkey the sundown law," Jack growled. My "What?" overlapped a timid male voice that said, "Hello?"

I realized that I was connected to a customer. In an icily calm voice I said, "Please put Mr. Jack back on the phone."

The telephone was transferred, and Jack came on with "Yeah?" I said, "What the hell is this all about?"

"Read this jerk the sundown law."

"What sundown law? What are you talking about?"

"This creep (how I cringed for the poor customer) bought a dog yesterday, took it home, killed it, and now he wants his fifty bucks back. I told him about the sundown law, but he don't believe me. You tell him."

"Jack, concentrate. WHAT IS THE SUNDOWN LAW?" I persisted.

Patronizingly, for the customer's benefit as well as mine, Jack laid down the sundown law. "You buy a pet, you got a problem, bring it back the same day, we'll talk about it. But comes sundown you haven't brought it back, it's yours, dead or alive. That's the sundown law." Then to the customer, "Get out of here, turkey."

I screamed his name at Jack.

"Yeah?"

"Jack, give that guy back his fifty bucks RIGHT NOW. I have never heard of the sundown law, the cops have never heard of the sundown law, and the judges have never heard of the sundown law. But we've all heard of fraud, and we've all heard of taking money under false pretenses, and we've all heard of selling some poor slob a derelict half dead with distemper that you snatched off the street in Richmond, Virginia."

"Baltimore," Jack corrected me. He had been enjoying my lecture. However, he chose that moment to hang up on me. I ran into him a month or so later and, against my better judgment, asked him if he had given the customer back his fifty dollars.

Never have I seen a happier man than Jack. "We made a deal." He waited for my inquiry, which forthcame.

"For another fifty bucks, I sold him a genuine Dalmatian worth three hundred easy."

"Baltimore?" I asked.

"Richmond," he beamed. "Great idea of yours."

Jack's sparkling bit of geographical repartee came to mind perhaps a year later when I opened my morning newspaper to find a handsome photograph of Jack, two other men, and a bear spread across three columns of the front page of the Metropolitan Section. The headline, "Pet Shop and Insurance Company Team Up to Enrich Our Zoo," was innocuous, but I knew Jack well enough to read on. The text disclosed that Jack had returned from his annual buying trip to Nepal with a Himalayan sun bear, described as a species of bear about the size and shape of a Virginia brown bear but distinctively marked with a broad white chevron on its hairy chest. Civic-minded Jack had ascertained that our zoo did not house a Himalayan sun bear. Learning this, Jack imaginatively contacted the Sun Life Insurance Company and put together a bestowal whereby Sun Life bought the bear from Jack and simultaneously donated it to the zoo which gratefully memorialized the gift with a bronze plaque identifying the beast as a Himalayan sun bear, demarking its native habitat, and identifying the Sun Life Insurance Company as the donor. The newspaper photograph featured Jack, the curator of our zoo, the president of Sun Life, and the bear, with an inset of the plaque.

Secure in the knowledge that Jack had never been west of St. Louis or east of Boston, I waited for the inevitable uncharacteristic telephone call. It came after the first heavy rain.

"You know about the sun bear?"

"Yes, I saw it in the paper."

"I want you to sue the bastard who sold me that bear."

"In Nepal?" I asked, playing it straight.

"In Lynchburg!" snorted Jack. "The son of a bitch charged me $100 and I had to bring my own crate, and now I have to pay 2,000 bucks for a real sun bear."

I asked Jack what had happened, and he told me. It seems that the fellow in Lynchburg had sworn on a large stack of Bible Belt bibles that the white acrylic paint which he had carefully stencilled onto the chest of Old Dan would never wear off, and that the chest hair of a mature Virginia brown bear stopped growing at the bear's maturity. The rest I knew from the newspaper article. However, when the rains came, the white acrylic chevron went, whereupon Old Dan was actually recognized by one of the zoo keepers. The curator quickly took Old Dan off display and telephoned Sun Life, giving it exactly one week to come up with the genuine article under pain of disclosure to the press. Sun Life gave Jack the same one week under pain of criminal proceedings; Jack found, bought, and surreptitiously supplied the zoo with the genuine article; Jack mercifully returned Old Dan to his native habitat, "gave him a good swift kick in the ass," and confronted his supplier, who fended Jack off with a shotgun. I counseled against litigation.

All of which, and a lot more, was preamble to Jack's entry into the big time, and my learning humility.

I had heard from a close friend whose father, Sam Harris, was a business broker, that Mr. Harris had put Jack on to a million dollar proposition, something really big that involved selling animals to the Government for medical testing purposes. Having received similar intelligence from a number of mutual acquaintances, I wasn't too surprised to get a telephone call from Jack at my home one evening. Not only was his voice the voice of doom, but he was even polite: Would I *please* come to Sam Harris's apartment *right now*? I walked into a veritable house of mourning. The only light in the room was supplied by one low-wattage desk lamp. In the shadows beyond the reach of its rays I could make out Harris, sunk motionless in an easy chair, and Jack, lying prostrate on a couch. I turned on a floor lamp, found a comfortable seat, and cheerily announced, "The meter is running, boys. What's the problem?"

It took a while for the story to come out, and a while longer for it to assume coherence, but what it boiled down to was this: In his ceaseless search for opportunity among the voluminous announcements of the United States Government's invitations for bids, Harris had noted that the United States Army required one hundred chimpanzees for medical testing at Walter Reed Army Medical Center. Knowing Jack and scenting opportunity, Harris had ferreted out the contracting officer, a Captain Wilmerding, and learned that since time immemorial, Watkins & Co., an animal importer in New York, had supplied virtually all of the Army's medical testing exotics, customarily by negotiated contract. However, a Congressional critic had stumbled across this pattern and persuaded the Pentagon that it was in the public interest that alternative suppliers be developed and encouraged to compete. Hence the invitation to bid.

Captain Wilmerding, who had become very friendly with the Watkins people, took an instant dislike to Harris and the fresh air he represented, but Harris went over his head and got the Pentagon to supply a list of potential sources of chimpanzees. Then Harris went to Jack, explained the deal, and put Jack to work. Through his wholesalers, Jack located a character named B. B. Barton in central Florida. B. B. Barton ran a combination alligator farm and gift shop whereat he led a life marked by both boredom and penury, in consequence of which he was instantly captivated by the idea of supplying chimpanzees to the United States Army. Somehow or other, Harris, Jack and Barton calculated that they could buy the chimpanzees in Africa for $100 apiece, ship them over for $20 apiece, and sell them to the Army for $650 apiece, thereby clearing $53,000, which they would divide $20,000 to Barton, $20,000 to Jack, and $13,000 to Harris. They had over-looked the Government's bonding requirement, but for $5,000 Harris was able to secure performance bonds from a major insurance company and they had duly submitted their bid. The bid, which was in Jack's name, was $20,000 lower than the only other bid, which came from the New York people, and it was the winning of the contract that sparked the citywide rumors that Jack was about to become a millionaire.

The telephone call to me was made two months and twenty days after the contract had been awarded to Jack. The reason it was made was that with ten days left in which to perform, Jack and Barton had not been able to purchase one single chimpanzee, although they had tried worldwide. Earlier that day, Harris had paid a call on Captain Wilmerding to tell him of his client's plight and request an extension. Captain Wilmerding had gleefully told Harris that under no circumstances would an extension be granted, and that he intended to contact the bonding company on the morrow. Harris had remonstrated vigorously, whereupon Captain Wilmerding had bodily expelled Harris from his office. Harris calculated that the New York people would proceed to fill the contract at a price of at least $1,000 per animal over Jack's bid, whereupon the bonding company would pay the Army $100,000 or more and come roaring after Jack, Barton, and Harris, all of whom had signed the bond application.

I made a brave attempt at salvation. The following morning I took Harris to the Pentagon, where I laid my clients' cards on the table and got a sixty-day extension. I then took Harris's list of possible sources and began telephoning all over the world. I lined up five possibilities, the most promising being a Mr. VanVroom in Amsterdam, but each time I appeared to connect, the source dried up. I gained a grudging admiration for the Watkins people in New York who were obviously and successfully cutting us off at every pass.

With two weeks of extension left and not a chimpanzee in

sight, I counseled the enlistment in our cause of the bonding company. Harris and Jack were horrified at the thought; I realized that they continued to cling to their original dream. I therefore suggested a summit conference by telephone with Barton and set it up for ten o'clock the next morning. Harris's nerves were too shattered to have him participate, so the following morning Jack came to my office and we put in a conference call to B. B. Barton and one Patrick Reilly, Barton's lawyer, who was located in Miami. It turned out that Barton had not previously consulted his lawyer, so I concisely summarized the facts for Mr. Reilly's benefit and he and I began to conduct a lawyerly colloquy respecting Government bids, surety bonds, and avenues of mitigation of damages. Reilly and I were having a rather good time, considering the circumstances, when B. B. Barton etched himself a permanent place in my psyche. I have never forgotten his words of interruption.

"SHUT UP, REILLY! SHUT UP, WOLF! LAWYERS ARE A DIME A DOZEN . . . . IT'S CHIMPANZEES THAT ARE HARD TO GET!

A week and a half later, with three days left for delivery and nary a chimp in sight, Jack came to my office for a last-ditch telephone conference with Barton, who at the twelfth hour claimed to be hot on the trail of fifteen chimps that just might have escaped the Watkins clamp. Jack was a changed man. It was clear to me that he was not devastated by the prospect of financial loss—I was sure that he would never pay a penny to the bonding company—but by the impending damage to his local prestige. Having no faith in Barton's claim, all Jack really hoped to accomplish was to enjoy a good cry with Barton, but his allergy to telephones had led him to my office so that I could put in the call for him. I dutifully dialed Barton's gift shop, where Mrs. Barton told me that B. B. had gone to New York and could probably be reached at the Eastern Air Lines freight counter at LaGuardia Field. I got the telephone number from New York Information and put in a station-to-station call. I reached a bright-voiced young man who identified his station, "Eastern Freight, can I help you?"

I inquired as to whether the young man knew a Mr. B. B. Barton, and if so, was Mr. Barton in the vicinity. The young man's response was nearly as memorable as Barton's outburst had been. "Oh, sure, I know Mr. Barton, but he's not here right now. He's gone out to get a sandwich with Mr. Watkins."

The only way I knew to give it to Jack was straight. I hung up; Jack looked up. I said, "Barton's gone out to get a sandwich with Mr. Watkins."

According to the bonding company, Captain Wilmerding paid Watkins & Co. $2,000 per chimpanzee, for a total of $200,000. The bonding company made up the difference and ended up owning an alligator farm and gift shop in central Florida. I'm sure Watkins & Co. saw to it that B. B. Barton couldn't have cared less.

"BUT WHERE IS YOUR HEART?"

Sidney Hirshon was a dutiful son, a competent baker, and a devotee of "family music." Not classical music, not popular music, but family music, the little snips of melody that he and his twice-widowed mother would invent in the evenings, after the six o'clock news had come over the radio and before Sidney's very early baker's bedtime.

After World War II began, their family music took on an Allied-wide patriotic cast, unintentionally close to bits and snatches of *The Last Time I Saw Paris, In an Old Dutch Garden By an Old Dutch Mill,* and *There'll Be Bluebirds Over the White Cliffs of Dover.* It was in the late autumn of 1941, shortly before Pearl Harbor and in the course of the annual vacation trip to New York that Sidney and his mother took to see Mother's brothers and sisters, that family music changed Sidney's life.

Mother was back at the hotel taking her afternoon nap when Sidney took his fateful stroll through Times Square. Humming family music, Sidney made his way north on Broadway from 44th Street to 46th Street, enjoying the hustle and the bustle, when a sharply dressed man pulled at his sleeve.

"What's that song you're humming?" the man demanded.

Nonplussed, Sidney mumbled, "I dunno, just family music."

"Hum it again," the man commanded. Sidney thought for a minute—his oeuvre was enormous—then remembered and obliged.

"Dum de dum de dum de dum," the man articulated, replacing Sidney's hums with *de dums.* "Right?"

"Yes," said Sidney, becoming vaguely excited. "That's right."

"It's sensational. You're a natural. Play any instruments?" the man asked.

"No," said Sidney.

"Read music?"

"No."

"Come with me, my boy; you'll wear diamonds." Saying which, the man led Sidney into the Brill Building—Tin Pan Alley itself— and up to his office.

The man reached into a desk drawer and took out a page of sheet music and a number 2 pencil. Repeating quite accurately "Dum de dum de dum de dum," the man drew in a treble clef and a bass clef, followed them with a bold 3/4, drew two eighth-notes at G below middle C, inscribed a bar followed by a half-note and a quarter-note at middle C, threw in another bar, drew a half-note at E, dropped down to middle C with a quarter-note, drew one more bar, and ascended to G above middle C where he ended with a magnificent dotted whole note (knowing Sidney wouldn't know the difference).

The man took his handiwork to the battered piano, put the newly minted music on the stand, hit the first two G's with one finger, and then accompanied the rest of Sidney's masterpiece with a mighty rolling bass.

"What's your name, Maestro?" the man asked Sidney.

"Sidney. Sidney Hirshon."

"A star is born, Sidney. A star is born." Saying which, the man played Sidney's creation again.

The musician in Sidney came out. "Try it softer," he told the man. "Sort of like bells."

The man obliged by crossing his left hand over his right hand to provide a tinkling accompaniment in the higher register. Sidney beamed. "That's perfect," he said.

Knowing when to close, the man leapt up from the piano and took another piece of paper from the desk drawer. "Got a wife, Sidney?" the man asked.

"No, I live with my mother."

"She musical?"

"She certainly is. I inherited it from her," Sidney said proudly.

"This here is a contract, Sidney, an honest-to-God contract. Take it home, go over it with your mother, you want to publish—*publish, Sidney*—you send it back to me with a measly five hundred bucks and I finish up your song, sent it back to you for the words..."

Sidney interrupted. "Mother will write the words!"

"Great, Sidney. You send me back the words and I'll deliver two thousand copies—*two thousand copies, Sidney*—to Bee Em Eye. BMI, they're the best, Sidney. Now run along, Sidney, I got work to do. I'm going to start finishing your song on spec, that's how much confidence I have, Sidney."

That's how it started, just that way. Sidney sent the man the signed contract and $500 from Mother's nest egg. The man sent Sidney thirty-two fleshed-out bars of music, Sidney's mother wrote the words, and true to his word, in May of 1942 the man delivered 2,000 copies of *London Bells Will Ring Again*, lyrics by Rose Weinar, music by Sidney Hirshon, to the offices of Broadcast Music, Inc. In an explosion of chutzpah, the man had legended every single copy "All Performance Rights Licensed Through Broadcast Music Incorporated" above a shield bearing the letters BMI. BMI never acknowledged receipt or otherwise contacted Sidney, although his name and address were included in each of the packages of music.

Ten years later, in the winter of 1952, Sidney took Mother to the movies to see "Moulin Rouge," starring José Ferrer as the misshapen Count Henri de Toulouse-Lautrec and Zsa Zsa Gabor as the lovely Jane Avril. They were happily lost in the beauty of the costumes, the tragedy and genius of the love-starved dwarf, and Offenbach's rollicking Can-Can music when lightning struck. The house lights (in the *Moulin Rouge*) went down, a simple spot illuminated Zsa Zsa, José started to capture her beauty on his tablecloth, and a single oboe began to play a haunting melody....Sidney's!!! Not exactly "dum de dum de dum de dum"—more like "de dum dah de dum"—but the same sequence of the same notes. Mother caught it, too; no question about it, she said, and that clinched it for Sidney.

In the morning Sidney went to the bakery and Mother went to the nearest music store where she bought a copy of the sheet music and the Percy Faith recording (which topped all the charts for the next several months). The sheet music, in brilliant red, bore the title *The Song From Moulin Rouge (Where Is Your Heart)*. The music was credited to Georges Auric, the movie was plugged as John Huston's *Moulin Rouge*, there was mention of José Ferrer, Zsa Zsa Gabor, and United Artists, and the publisher was prominently identified as Broadcast Music, Inc. The phonograph record was entitled *Where is Your Heart?* and subtitled in parentheses *(The Song from Moulin Rouge)*. Mother then called the Bar Association and got the names of three copyright lawyers; the third one took the case.

Sidney's lawyer chose to sue United Artists first. The trial commenced in the United States District Court for the District of Columbia on January 27, 1958, before a jury of nine whites and three Negroes (as blacks were then known), Judge James Morris presiding. During the course of the five-week trial, *Moulin Rouge* was shown in full three times and the Percy Faith recording was played fifty times, all for the elucidation of the judge and the jury.

Proof of plagiarism is essayed by proving access and similarity. The concepts are reciprocal in that if similarity is nigh-perfect, the claimant doesn't have to make a strong showing of access, while if access is peculiarly available, similarity can be a lot less than perfect identity. In the law of literary property, the question is not identity of product; the question is theft. Generally speaking, it's one of intent (although Judge Learned Hand attributed "unconscious plagiarism" to Jerome Kern in the case of *Fisher v. Dillingham*!).

Sidney was on the witness stand for four days. Could he read music? No. Could he write music? No. Could he play music? No. But Sidney was dogged: He could *hum* music, music of his own invention, family music. He told his Times Square story with an utterly credible ingenuousness. There in the United States Courthouse, in the majesty of the courtroom, nervous but forthright, it became crystal clear that Sidney had no idea, would never have an idea, that his guardian angel might have been a hustler who made a parlous living searching out Sidneys up and down Broadway and keeping out of jail by actually delivering the goods (at a cost to himself of $50 per 2,000 copies, delivered).

Then began the battle of the experts. Sidney's expert was a charming black woman who was the Chairman of the Department of Music at Howard University. She smartly disclaimed any similarity between Sidney's *London Bells* and Auric's *Moulin Rouge except for* the first seven notes of *London Bells* and the first five notes of *Moulin Rouge.*

She went to the piano which had been installed in the courtroom and played as she sang. "G - G - C - C - E - C - G—*London Bells,*" she announced to the jury. "G - C (stretched out) - E - C - G—*Moulin Rouge.*" She repeated the exercise three times, then resumed the witness stand and gave the jury an impressive history of Haydn leaning on Bach, and Beethoven leaning on Mozart, and Brahms leaning on Schubert, following which she went back to the piano and showed the jury how close "leaning on" came to "copying from."

So much for similarity. Sidney's case closed with his evidence of access, which consisted of deposition testimony, read to the jury, proving without question that 2,000 copies of *London Bells Will Ring Again* were unsolicitedly and unceremoniously dumped on the floor of the reception area in the offices of Broadcast Music, Inc., in New York City on the 5th day of May, in the year 1942.

Defending United Artists and, on the remove, BMI, we had an unlimited budget and access to the stars. We decided that a star-studded defense would backfire, so we declined to use the great names of music and musicology which were available to us and went with the Chairman of the Music Department of American University, the learned and sincere (and white—more about that soon) James Maclean. Professor Maclean made mincemeat of the idea that anyone could *own* five notes as literary property, and showed the jury that the notes in question were the stuff of every bugle call ever written. The judge jumped in to say that he remembered them from Somewhere in France in World War I. We followed Professor Maclean with the French Military Attaché, in full brigadier's regalia, who reinforced the bugle call theme, and then called to the witness stand Monsieur Georges Auric, world-renowned composer of classical music, one of "Les Six" of Roaring Twenties fame, Directeur of the Paris Opera....and composer of *The Song From Moulin Rouge.*

In his late sixties, on crutches and in obvious pain from a recent varicose vein operation, and testifying in French through an interpreter, M. Auric told the jury the fascinating history of *The Song.*

Auric testified that one evening in 1950, while he and his wife were dining in their elegant apartment on the Île St. Louis, the telephone rang. The caller was his old friend John Huston, who said that he was in Paris and asked if he could pay a call "on a matter of gravest import." Having sold music to Hollywood before, and knowing and trusting Huston, Auric recognized the code for the possibility of big money and assured Huston that he would welcome him with open arms.

Huston came to Auric's apartment, Huston and the Aurics had a cognac, Madame Auric retired, and Huston came right to the point. [Here Auric provided the jury with one sentence of Frenglish.] "Georges, open le tronc."

I interrupted with a question aimed midway between Auric and the interpreter. "Open what?" Independent of Auric the interpreter said, "Mr. Auric says that Mr. Huston asked him to open the trunk." Sidney's lawyer hopped up to object to the interpreter's independent testimony, but the judge sat him down with a baleful glare. Taking advantage of the judicial visage, I said to Auric, "Continuez, s'il vous plait."

Auric asked Huston why he wanted him to open the trunk. Huston said that United Artists had engaged him to direct a big-budget spectacular starring José Ferrer and Zsa Zsa Gabor for which Huston needed some appropriate French music. Appropriate to what, asked Auric. Huston put on a brave face and said that Ferrer's dedication to his art was so vast that he had agreed to walk on his knees, where walking was necessary, in order to do justice to the Gallic courage of le Compte Henri de Toulouse-Lautrec.

Auric testified that Auric had then said, "Merde! You're not doing that old chestnut again?" [The interpreter left the "merde" untranslated, which was fine with the judge.]

"Yes, but magnificently, Georges," said Huston.

"Why do you need me? Offenbach's Can-Can has just gone into the public domain, where it won't cost you a sou," said Auric.

"We know that, Georges, but I see the film running about one hundred and fifty minutes and I don't think that the audience can take more than twenty minutes of the Can-Can. We need something fresh and original; please, Georges, get the trunk."

Auric testified that he grudgingly went into his study and got the trunk. He showed the jury with his hands that the trunk was a box about three feet wide, two feet deep, and eighteen inches high. He said that he put it on the floor and opened it to reveal hundreds of pieces of paper of all sorts, sheet music, music paper, letters, envelopes, napkins, doilies, even a few paper plates, all with music scribbled on them.

Auric testified that Huston beamed and said, "The trunk is even fuller than I remembered, Georges. Find me something for *Moulin Rouge*."

Auric said that he and Huston sat for three hours while he selected possible candidates and hummed them to Huston. At the end of this exercise they had come up with perhaps twenty possibilities, whereupon Auric had gone to the piano and vamped them all, after which Huston picked two songs which were in manuscript and one which had actually been printed as sheet music.

At that point in his testimony, Auric paused for effect, then spat out something unprintable which the interpreter translated as "That stupid Zsa Zsa!"

Auric then digressed, but I had no cause to interrupt and Sidney's lawyer didn't dare. Looking from juror to juror, Auric testified that the best of the three songs, the most Gallic, thereafter polished, printed, and dispatched to Hollywood, could not be used in the movie because "that stupid Zsa Zsa" was unable to move her lips fast enough to synchronize with Betty Smith's singing.

Leaving the jurors a moment in which to look confused, an effect he obviously intended, Auric went on to explain that Zsa Zsa couldn't sing two notes in correct succession, to the end that one Betty Smith had done all of the singing ostensibly performed by Zsa Zsa in *Moulin Rouge*, but that she was "too stupid" to mouth his best song.

I got Auric back on the track by interposing a question. "What was the song in the trunk that had already been printed?"

Auric relaxed the intensity he had brought to his defamation of Zsa Zsa, shifted in the witness chair, and got back on the track.

He testified that in the winter of 1940, during what was known as the Phony War, he had written a song entitled "Adieu, Mon Copain" for performance in a French motion picture starring the celebrated French actress Madame Arletti. He then treated the jury to a snatch of *The Song from Moulin Rouge* with the original lyric, croaking "Adieu, mon copain, adieu, l'aventure."

The interpreter duly translated into "Goodbye, my pal, goodbye, adventure." Sensing an impending digression and anxious to defer it, I threw in a question.

"Was the French movie made?"

"Ah," breathed Auric. That movie, he testified, went into musical rehearsal as scheduled, on a historic day in May 1940. With "Adieu, Mon Copain" in hand, he met Madame Arletti and the film's music director at a Parisian recording studio for a runthrough. He sat at the piano with the music open before him, Madame Arletti stood a few feet away with her copy of the song, the music director sat across the room smoking cigarettes and listening attentively, and they began their rehearsal. "Half way through," said Auric, "I encountered competition."

Auric sat back, stared at the ceiling, and was silent for perhaps thirty seconds. He then leaned forward; I noticed that the jurors did likewise.

"My competition was the sound of German guns," he announced in a voice of doom. "I looked at Arletti, we both looked at the music director, the director shrugged his shoulders in despair, I took the sheets of music from the piano, and we all left the studio. I went to the south of France, where I joined the Resistance. I never saw Arletti again....except at the cinema."

Auric sat back again; he had the faculty of adjusting the level of drama in the courtroom by repositioning his backbone. He ended his direct testimony with a matter-of-fact recital that "Adieu, Mon Copain" had gone into "le tronc" where it had rested until he retrieved it for John Huston and *Moulin Rouge*.

In desperation, Sidney's lawyer hazarded an "Are you sure?" cross-examination. "Are you sure it's the same song?" "Are you sure you wrote it in 1940?" And finally, "Are you sure that BMI didn't send you a copy of *London Bells Will Ring Again?*" Auric not only erupted in predictable rage at this last suggestion, but when he finished the securing of his own honor and the resurrection of the glory of France, he then launched an unsolicited but unquenchable tirade directed at Percy Faith! As he segued directly from his counterattack on Sidney's lawyer into his fulminations against Faith, he made it clear that he would not brook interruption and that he intended to air this last grievance before all of his new friends on the jury.

In the middle of his fulminations, which the interpreter was having great trouble keeping up with, Auric suddenly pulled himself out of the witness chair, seized and adjusted his crutches, and hobbled to the courtroom piano. I sneaked a look at the judge. It was clear that he did not intend to miss a syllable or a note of whatever it was that Auric wanted to say or play. The judge nodded at the interpreter, who correctly took this as a signal that he should stand by the piano and continue interpreting.

Auric did a rapid rundown of *The Song*, stopping at the begin-

ning of the last line, which in the Percy Faith recording reads
"....But where is your heart?"

Auric instructed the interpreter to advise the jury that his composition, as written by him and as played in the film, had an
unresolved ending consisting of the notes he then played: D - E -
F - E - D - E - D - C - D - E - F - E - D

He let the final D fade away for perhaps ten seconds and then
announced "Trés jolie!" He then changed his expression from total
approbation to sneering detestation and told the jury that the
unspeakable Percy Faith had castrated, yes, castrated his lovely
song by shortening the plaintive irresolution thusly:

D - E - F - E - D - C

He then muttered something sharp and obviously unpleasant
in French. Before the interpreter could translate, the judge turned
to Sidney's lawyer and asked him, in a tone which commanded
the negative, if he had any more questions of Monsieur Auric.
Sidney's lawyer quickly disclaimed possessing any more questions,
and without bothering to ask me if I had any redirect examination, the judge offered Auric a very formal expression of gratitude
on behalf of the parties, the lawyers, the jury, and American justice, adjourned Court for the day, and swiftly left the bench.

Auric sat at the piano until the jury had filed out of the courtroom, when he turned and looked at Sidney for the first time. He
then astounded Sidney and all counsel by saying, in heavily accented English, "Poor leetle man." Sidney fled, his lawyer followed,
and we of the defense saw M. Auric to the limousine provided for
him by the French Ambassador.

The next morning, the jury was treated to closing arguments
and comprehensive judicial instruction, and retired to reach its
verdict. Sidney's lawyer was game to the last in front of the jury,
but once the jurors had retired, he predicted a verdict for the defendant in no more than ten minutes.

Three hours later, we were still awaiting a verdict. The judge
returned to the bench and communicated his impatience to the
jury via the marshal. A further three hours later, the judge's pa-

tience snapped and he ordered the marshal to bring the jury back into the courtroom. He asked the foreman if they had reached a unanimous verdict. The foreman replied that they had not and that he did not think that they could.

Not bothering to contain his manifest ire, the judge there and then declared a mistrial, invited counsel to interview the jury, and left the bench.

I caught the eye of one of the woman jurors and walked over to a far corner of the courtroom, where she joined me.

"What in the world happened?" I asked her.

"It was unbelievable," she said, "and it was all so awful."

"Well," I persisted, "what happened?"

"We went into the jury room and that sweet-faced idiot standing over there in the red hat announced, 'We have nothing to deliberate. That twerp Hirshon didn't write a single note of *Moulin Rouge.*'

"One of the colored men—that tall, light-skinned one talking to Hirshon's lawyer—said that he thought we should at least talk about what the expert witnesses had said." My juror paused and then said, "Mr. Wolf, you won't believe what happened next!"

"What did?" I asked.

"Sweet-Face turned to the colored man and said 'I'm not going to spend five minutes listening to you tell me what a wonderful witness that lying nigger-woman was!'

"The colored man and the other two colored men on the jury sat up as if they had been stung by bees—the rest of us were too flabbergasted to say a word—and the colored man narrowed his eyes to slits, Mr. Wolf, and said, 'Lady, we don't have to talk about a single thing. Just tell me how you're voting, and you can be damned sure that whichever way that is, I'm voting the other way, whether we're here for five minutes or five weeks.'

"When the rest of us recovered, we held our own meeting and then some of us tried to get Sweet-Face to apologize and some of us apologized for her and tried to persuade the colored men that they had a civic duty and ought to perform it. But it was hopeless.

All Sweet-Face would say was, 'Did you hear what that man said to me?' and all the colored man said was 'Do you expect us to pretend that bitch never opened her mouth?'"

About a week later, we received notice from the Court that the case would be retried in the Fall. Sidney's lawyer called to say that he had advanced $7,500 in expenses for Sidney, which Sidney couldn't repay, so Sidney had authorized him to drop the lawsuit if United Artists would clear up his obligation. We passed this intelligence along to United Artists and BMI, together with our plagiarized slogan, "Millions for defense, but not one cent for tribute." Word came back that as the millions for defense would go to us, and as no one could predict what a jury would do, we were commanded to pay Sidney and his lawyer $7,500 in return for full releases of both United Artists and BMI bearing Sidney's signature and the appropriate attestation by a notary public duly and currently commissioned in the District of Columbia.

We had no choice but to acquiesce in our clients' instructions. I signalled our acquiescence by a letter to the clients in which I acknowledged that their decision was monetarily sensible, but it inspired a question that I wanted to put to both of them. My question appears as the title of this tale.

"THE NAKED GUITARIST"

Jean-Pierre Jumez was a handsome young Parisian guitarist possessed of great charm, a large talent in his chosen field of classical guitar, and the good sense to know when to keep his clothes on.

He was in his early twenties when his government appointed him an ambassador of French culture, an appointment which carried with it a stipend sufficient to enable him to roam the world holding master classes and giving concerts, thereby reflecting glory on the Motherland. So doing, he picked up seven or eight languages, had a wonderful time, and enhanced the image of France as still a seedbed of Western artistry and art.

Following a successful appearance in Wellington, New Zealand, Jean-Pierre was approached by two members of his audience who introduced themselves as the proprietors of a local recording company called Kiwi Records. At their invitation, the next morning Jean-Pierre donned his tuxedo and repaired to their studio where he recorded twelve numbers, posed for a jacket cover photograph, provided biographical material for the liner notes, and signed a royalty contract giving Kiwi Records full right, title, and interest in and to the performance just recorded. That afternoon he flew to Tahiti, where he felt very much at home.

At the conclusion of that tour, Jean-Pierre returned to Paris, where there awaited him a 33 rpm phonograph record housed in a jacket bearing a dignified black-and-white photograph of himself, clean-shaven and tuxedo-clad, strumming his guitar. The legend on the jacket read simply *Jean-Pierre Jumez*. The back of the record jacket carried the liner notes written by Kiwi from the biographical data Jean-Pierre had provided in Wellington, together with Kiwi's claim to worldwide copyright.

This phonograph record constituted the last communication Jean-Pierre ever received from Kiwi Records, and he soon forgot all about the recording he had made in New Zealand.

Two years and two world circumnavigations later, still an ambassador of French culture, Jean-Pierre made his way to Denver, Colorado, where he was scheduled to give a master class to the Denver guitar club, followed the succeeding evening by a concert at the University of Denver. After he gave the master class, one of the local guitarists came up to him and said, "I just bought your latest recording, Jean-Pierre; it's wonderful!"

When Jean-Pierre disclaimed any knowledge of a "latest recording" on sale in the United States—all of his records other than the Kiwi recording had been pressed and sold only in Europe—the student said that she would bring her acquisition to the concert. The concert was a great success; afterwards, there was the usual party hosted by the guitar club. As she had promised, the master class student came up to Jean-Pierre, complimented him on his performance, and handed him her recent acquisition.

With a slap to his forehead and an anguished "Mon Dieu!" Jean-Pierre collapsed into a nearby chair.

What the lady had handed him was a recording of the music he had recorded in Wellington, New Zealand, packaged much differently than by Kiwi. The record jacket, in full color, bore the title "The Nimble Fingers of Jean Pierre Jumez" in large print, upper right quadrant. The rest of the jacket was filled with an unbordered photograph of a headless man dressed from bushy beard to waist in formal wear, seated in a chair. He held a guitar on his lap, with the upper rather than the lower belly of the guitar between his legs and the fingers of his right hand midlap, extending *through* the strings to God knew where. His thighs and knees dominated the bottom third of the jacket cover.

His thighs and knees were bare.

Jean-Pierre bought this record just before leaving Denver the next morning. The liner notes on the reverse of the jacket were the very ones that Kiwi had printed, but the copyright notice made no mention of Kiwi Records, proclaiming that the recording was from the Westminster Gold Collection produced by ABC Records, Inc., a subsidiary of the American Broadcasting Company.

Jean-Pierre's American tour took him next to Seattle, then to Portland and San Francisco, and finally to Los Angeles, the home of the West Coast headquarters of ABC and its subsidiaries. When he reached L.A., he went immediately to the offices of ABC Records, gave his name, identified himself as an ABC recording artist, and asked to see the man in charge.

He was told by the gorgeous receptionist that there would be a short wait, as Mr. John Franklin Madison was extremely busy. He was left to cool his heels for an hour and a half—plainly, he was expected to lose patience and leave—but as his heels became cooler, his temper became hotter, and he determined to wait all day if necessary.

Sensing Jean-Pierre's determination, Miss Gorgeous mumbled a few words into a telephone and then told Jean-Pierre that Mr. Madison had cleared away five minutes and would now see him. He was escorted into a magnificent office and introduced to the most arrogant human being he had ever met.

Furious but composed, Jean-Pierre told Mr. Madison his story. Madison, well prepared, responded by telling Jean-Pierre that ABC had purchased the rights to the recording from Kiwi Records and had spent a considerable sum of money on the jacket cover to make it attractive to a young audience; he therefore assumed that Jean-Pierre had come to ABC to express his appreciation for his inclusion in the Westminster Gold Collection.

Jean-Pierre exploded in rage. He demanded the immediate recall of all unsold records, the destruction of all of the recalled record jackets, and the reissuance of the record with a different title and in a redesigned jacket preapproved by him.

A recall is out of the question, responded Madison; however, *if* sales of the present recording warrant a second pressing, ABC *might* be willing to redesign the cover for that pressing, but Monsieur Jumez should keep in mind that the title of the record could in no event be changed because it was fixed in ABC's catalogue. But perhaps Monsieur Jumez would accept a cash payment of $1,500 to resolve the entire matter.

Before Jean-Pierre could react, the receptionist opened the office door to announce that Mr. Madison's next appointment had arrived. Jean-Pierre was unceremoniously dismissed.

I filed *Jumez v. ABC Records, Inc.* in the Federal Courthouse on Foley Square in New York City, alleging in the Complaint that Jean-Pierre had been defamed, that he was the victim of an invasion of his privacy, and that he was entitled to punitive as well as compensatory damages. As the judge later explained to the jury, under the law, "invasion of privacy" includes the tort of placing a person in a false light before the public, which is what I alleged ABC had done to Jean-Pierre by suggesting that in order to sell records and thereby make money, he had posed for the jacket cover naked from the waist down with his fingers wriggling toward his upper lap between the strings of a mislocated guitar.

ABC, represented by a mammoth Wall Street law firm, filed an Answer denying all allegations and demanding that the lawsuit be dismissed.

The trial began on a Monday morning in September before Judge Lawrence Pierce and a jury of six persons in a courtroom on the twenty-eighth floor of the Federal Courthouse. My only witness was Jean-Pierre. He told the jury his life story in delightfully accented English, switching to his native tongue only when he slapped his forehead and quoted his "Mon Dieu!" As he described the anguish ABC Records had brought him, his life abruptly turning from delight to horror, with his career threatened with oblivion and his ambassadorship threatened with termination, the jurors appeared to suffer with him. I closed my case, and it was ABC's turn.

ABC's lawyer called three witnesses. His first witness was the National Sales Manager of ABC Records. This witness painted Jean-Pierre as an obscure minor talent whose recording ABC had bought only because Kiwi Records had thrown him in on a deal involving the purchase of early recordings made at Kiwi by the great Maori soprano Kiri Te Kanawa before she became one of grand opera's most luminous stars. On cross-examination I asked the witness if, when he was busily selling Jean-Pierre's record throughout the country, he knew whether the artist was dead or alive. No, he responded, he did not. I paused for a moment, then asked, "Did you *care*?"

ABC's lawyer jumped to his feet to object, but he was too late. The witness had replied "Nah" before Judge Pierce sustained the objection. "No further questions, if Your Honor please," said I. How heartless can you be, ABC?

ABC's next witness was Peter Whorf, the designer of the jacket covers of most of the one hundred and fifty or so records in the Westminster Gold Collection. It was plain that his testimonial assignment was to further denigrate Jean-Pierre's talent. His approach to this hatchet job was to explain to the jury that the Westminster Gold Collection had been created by ABC Records to attract college-age youths and young marrieds to classical music at cut-rate prices. Engaged to work on the project from its planning stage, Whorf had proposed that each jacket cover be a photograph mildly spoofing the music within. The music itself, Whorf told the jury, had cost ABC very little money; the Collection, Whorf testified, consisted largely of the works of second-rate composers performed by second-rate musicians and purchased by ABC on the cheap, filled out by the reissue of old performances from ABC's library, all gussied up by the striking new jacket covers.

This testimony was not entirely lacking in verisimilitude, but I was ready for it when Judge Pierce invited me to cross-examine. Having made a note of Whorf's exact words, I asked him to confirm his previous testimony that the Westminster Gold Collection consisted predominately of works by second-rate composers performed by second-rate musicians. He confirmed. I then handed him Westminster Gold Release No. 47, a jacket cover consisting of a photograph of two men playing tennis, and asked him if he had designed that cover. He drew within himself a little—he knew what was coming—and answered that in fact he had. I had him read the jury the title of No. 47, "Julian Bream Plays J. S. Bach." (Thus the tennis players on the cover.) He did so firmly and with courage; he had decided to resign himself to his fate. I asked him if the J. S. Bach named on the jacket cover was by any chance Johann Sebastian Bach; the very same, he assured me and the jury.

"Do you consider Johann Sebastian Bach to be a second-rate composer?" I asked gently.

"It's my personal opinion," he replied evenly, "that Bach is the greatest composer of them all."

"And Julian Bream....," I began, but Whorf interrupted me and addressed the jury in an instructive voice. "Andrés Segovia and Julian Bream are the finest classical guitarists alive today."

I put No. 47 aside and picked up No. 113, which featured a photograph of a baseball player in full uniform, holding a bat. It was entitled "Virgil Fox's Greatest Hits." I asked Professor Whorf to tell the jury who E. Power Biggs was; he advised his six pupils that E. Power Biggs was unquestionably the greatest organist in the world. "And where do you place Virgil Fox?" I asked. "Just under Biggs," he responded. "Nobody else can touch them." "And whose music is Fox playing on this record?" I asked. "Bach, of course," replied Whorf.

And so it went with six more records from the Westminster Gold Collection, world-class talent playing superb compositions by the greatest composers who ever lived. On redirect examination, ABC's lawyer elicited Whorf's opinion that the plaintiff's recording was not on a par with those as to which he had just testified. I did not reexamine.

Judge Pierce excused Whorf and called a welcome recess. I went out in the hallway to smoke a cigarette. Peter Whorf came up to me trailed by ABC's lawyer, put out his hand, and said with a laugh, "You sure picked 'em." When I shook his hand and grinned back at him, he said, "Would you agree that the other hundred and forty or so are turkeys?" I replied, "Not until the case is over!"

Judge Pierce reconvened the proceedings and ABC's lawyer

asked the Clerk to call the next witness to the stand. The door to the courtroom swung open and in strode John Franklin Madison, the Mr. Madison of L.A. fame, obviously present to testify as to Jean-Pierre's ingratitude at his inclusion in the Westminster Gold Collection and as to the outrageousness of Jean-Pierre's demands. He marched imperiously forward, giving Jean-Pierre not the courtesy of a glance, and took the oath. Before Mr. Madison was asked the first question, Judge Pierce intervened.

"It's four thirty," he announced, "and I think we've had enough for one day. We'll resume at ten o'clock tomorrow morning."

ABC's lawyer rose and addressed the Court. "Your Honor, Mr. Madison has flown in this afternoon from Los Angeles, and he *must* be back by tomorrow afternoon."

"All right," said His Honor. "We'll resume at nine thirty. Good day, ladies and gentlemen." So saying, he left the bench.

I had barely set foot in the hallway and lit up when ABC's lawyer rushed up to me accompanied by Mr. Madison. "Bill Wolf," the lawyer addressed me, "I would like you to meet John Franklin Madison."

The lawyer continued, "As I indicated to Judge Pierce, Mr. Madison *must* catch the eleven o'clock plane to Los Angeles tomorrow morning. I'll only have him on the stand for fifteen minutes; you won't need more time than that for cross-examination, will you?" Madison's face was frozen in arrogance; he was staring over my left shoulder, not deigning to look at inconsequential me.

I needed him to look at me, so I said to him, softly and with as obsequious a smile as I could summon up, "You *must* be at LaGuardia Field by eleven?"

I got back a haughty, "Absolutely," but he looked at me.

Still soft of voice and slightly smiling, I said, "You will be asked three questions by my friend here, your lawyer. I will then ask you five questions on cross-examination. Let me tell you what *his* questions will be, and what *my* questions will be, and the answers you will give to each question."

I paused; ABC's lawyer drew in his breath. I continued; my voice did not remain soft.

"*Because*, you arrogant son of a bitch, if you stray one syllable from my script—and that goes for your buddy here, too—I'll keep you on the witness stand till Christmas!"

Madison bit his lower lip, hard. "What are the questions?"

"And the answers," I reminded him.

"And the answers," he echoed.

"Your pal here will ask you your name and occupation; you will give them. Then he will ask you if Jean-Pierre came to your office in Los Angeles to express his enormous distress at the "Nimble Fingers" jacket cover. Your answer will be yes. Then he will ask you how long Jean-Pierre was in your office. You will answer that he was in your office for five minutes; you will add that you were very busy that day. Your lawyer will then say that he has no further questions.

"I will ask you if you suspected what he wanted, and had him wait in your anteroom for an hour and a half in the hope that he would go away. You will answer yes. I will ask you if he appeared to be greatly distressed by what ABC had done to him in selling his performance in a false and obscene album jacket. You will answer that he was greatly distressed. I will ask you if you tried to buy him off with the suggestion that perhaps he could be paid fifteen hundred dollars. You will answer yes. I will ask you if he expressed any interest in accepting fifteen hundred dollars. You will answer no. I will ask you if you had him shown the door five minutes after he came into your office. You will answer yes.

"That will be your testimony, every word of which happens to be the truth.

"Yes or no, Mr. Madison?"

"Of course," he said quietly. He had shed his arrogance like a snake sheds its skin.

We started at exactly nine thirty the following morning, and I got him off the witness stand by ten sharp. He looked at his wristwatch, rose from the stand, and then did a very strange thing. He put out his hand. As I shook it, he said with utmost sincerity, "Thank you very much, Mr. Wolf."

The jury retired to deliberate around four o'clock in the afternoon of the sixth day of the trial. In giving the jurors his instructions, Judge Pierce had directed them to return a special verdict, which meant that they were to respond to a set of eight specific questions. After the jurors had left the courtroom, Judge Pierce said that he assumed that no verdict would be rendered that day, but he would wait until eight o'clock before adjourning for the evening.

The jury surprised us all by returning the verdict at 6:30. The bailiff rounded me up from the hallway and ABC's lawyer from the men's room, and we resumed our places at the trial tables, the plaintiff's table at a right angle to the front of the jury box and the defendant's table immediately to the rear of the plaintiff's table. Judge Pierce asked the foreman of the jury if the jurors had reached a unanimous verdict; the foreman replied that they had. The judge then directed the Clerk to read the first special verdict question.

"Do you, the jury, find that the defendant, ABC Records, defamed the plaintiff, Jean-Pierre Jumez, in publishing the phonograph record album entitled 'The Nimble Fingers of Jean Pierre Jumez'?"

The foreman waited a moment, then said in a loud, clear voice, "No."

My heart plunged past the lobby of the Federal Courthouse, twenty-seven floors below, and continued until it reached the bedrock on which Manhattan stands. I could not see ABC's lawyer, who sat behind me, but I could *feel* him growing ten feet tall.

"That disposes of the second, third, and fourth questions," Judge Pierce announced. He turned to his Clerk. "Please read the fifth question."

"Do you, the jury, find that the defendant, ABC Records, invaded the privacy of the plaintiff, Jean-Pierre Jumez, by placing him in a false light before the public in publishing the phonograph record album entitled 'The Nimble Fingers of Jean Pierre Jumez'?"

Again the foreman waited a moment. Then he said "Yes."

My cardiovascular resuscitation took a few seconds to kick in. It was in process as Judge Pierce nodded to the Clerk to continue reading the questions.

"What sum of money do you award Jean-Pierre Jumez as compensatory damages?"

The foreman did not hesitate. "Fifty thousand dollars."

"Do you find that the actions of the defendant, ABC Records, were malicious, wanton, or reckless, and entitle the plaintiff, Jean-Pierre Jumez, to an award of punitive damages?"

"Yes."

"What sum of money do you award Jean-Pierre Jumez as punitive damages?"

"Ninety thousand dollars."

My cardiac recovery was more than complete.

Judge Pierce thanked and dismissed the jurors, who filed out of the courtroom to resume their normal lives. Then he addressed the lawyers.

"Gentlemen, I congratulate you both on a job very well done. I have serious doubts that I should let the punitive damage award stand; heedlessness is not malice. I will accept an oral motion from the defendant for judgment *non obstante verdicto* on the point—" ABC's lawyer said, "If Your Honor please," "—and await defendant's brief and plaintiff's reply. Good night, gentlemen."

I explained to Jean-Pierre that the punitive damages award was extremely tenuous. He couldn't have cared less and left the courtroom in ecstasy. ABC's lawyer came up to me as I was packing my briefcase, congratulated me, and surprised me with a request I found extraordinary.

"I've tried hundreds of lawsuits," he said, "and win or lose, I've always ended up disliking the opposing lawyer.

"You were mighty slick with Whorf and mighty rough with Madison, but Goddammit, I like your style. Will you have dinner with me at The Palm—" he looked at his watch "—at nine thirty?"

We had a great dinner. I went back to Washington the next morning. Six weeks later, after the briefing was done, Judge Pierce set aside the award of punitive damages and ABC Records sent me a check for fifty thousand dollars. I was disappointed that "John Franklin Madison" wasn't the signature on ABC's check.

"MARTHA"

The relegation of radio from America's prime time entertainment to background music and shock jockeys has left few people who remember Arthur Tracy, but he was once one of the best-known personalities in the land. During the 1930s, for a fabled fifteen minutes just before Amos 'n' Andy, all America listened to Tracy's rolling baritone introduce "The Street Singer" with his unforgettable rendition of his theme song, "*Martha....RRRambling RRRose of the Wild Wood....*" Tracy's R's rolled like waves hastening to crash upon a rugged shore.

Some time around 1940 Tracy invested a substantial amount of money in a garden apartment development in Washington, D. C., called Brentwood Village. The development was very successful, so when Tracy's associates sold their interests to a New York group called Nassau Management Company, Tracy decided to retain his interest in the project. The roof fell in on the Nassau Management people in connection with an unrelated project, and they hastened into bankruptcy and in several cases into jail.

Thus when a client of mine appeared with a problem involving a large Brentwood Village obligation to him which was overdue, we searched for a creditworthy obligor, and lo! the city records showed Arthur Tracy as a partner in the project. I located him in New York City and wrote several letters inquiring as to his status in the project. My letters went unanswered, so my client directed me to file suit against Tracy.

Tracy was represented by a large New York law firm; his responsive pleading denied liability on the grounds that the only role he had played was the most honorable one of stepping forward to pay current running expenses of Brentwood Village in order to maintain it as home for the hundreds of people who lived there, and that he had no responsibility whatsoever for any past misallocation or misappropriation of funds by Nassau Management.

As the obligation to my client antedated Nassau Management's collapse, it appeared that if Tracy had in fact played no role during the bad times, he had no obligation to my client, but that if he had participated even innocently in the management while the Nassau people were in charge, he might well be liable to pay my client from his personal funds.

I tried to make the necessary determination without further invocation of the majesty of the law, but Tracy's lawyers were less than ceremonious in advising me that their client deeply resented being sued, and had instructed them to engage in no discussions of any kind with me until we met in the courtroom.

I had no intention of waiting that long to make the necessary determination, and the Federal Rules of Civil Procedure afforded me the opportunity to accelerate the process. I served Tracy with a notice of deposition upon oral examination *duces tecum*, requiring him to attend and give testimony under oath at an appointed date and time in the offices of a friend of mine in New York, and further requiring him to bring with him for my scrutiny all Brentwood Village cancelled checks bearing his signature.

He appeared as required....and did he appear! He was wearing a tan suit with trousers creased to a knife-edge, a beautifully figured necktie resting against a silk white-on-white shirt, a yellow waistcoat perfectly matching his blond toupee, and fawn- colored spats, carrying an umbrella which matched the spats. Accompanying him was his lawyer, Robert Stern.

He bristled with impatience, peremptorily commanding me and the court reporter to get on with it! I purposely conducted my examination at a leisurely pace, taking him through the history of Brentwood Village from the Year One and impassively bearing the brunt of his frequent attacks, which took the form of fulsomely complimenting Stern each time he registered an objection on the record—"Well said, Robert," and the like—and then turning to me and literally snarling, "Get on with it, Wolf, I've got better things to do with my time."

Taking *my* time, I eventually came to the Nassau Management collapse and the voluntary takeover of current obligations of Brentwood Village by Tracy, and politely requested that he produce the required cancelled checks. Tracy turned to Stern and resentfully asked him, "Do I have to, Robert?" Stern, picking up his deportment from Tracy's, condescendingly replied, "It will save time, Arthur," whereupon Tracy said, "Well, then, give them to him," articulating these words with a full-court sneer.

Stern fished in his briefcase and dropped about a hundred checks on the conference table. I riffled through them, interested mainly in the dates, and quickly satisfied myself that Tracy was not only wholly innocent of any skullduggery but that he had done exactly what he had claimed, which was to pay current obligations to keep the project afloat. Clearly he owed my client nothing. But just as clearly he now owed me a great deal, and I determined that he was going to pay....my way.

I picked up the top check on the pile and asked the reporter to mark it as plaintiff's Exhibit 1 for identification. She complied, the process taking approximately a minute and a half. I then had Tracy identify his signature, read the date into the record, specify the payee of the check, and relate the purpose for which the check had been drawn. By the time I had repeated this procedure for the next three checks in the pile, Tracy's face was a mask of fury. He could see that the examination, check by check, was going to take at least two more hours, and his gorge had risen to the heavens. I looked him in the eye and sprang my trap.

"Mr. Tracy, my client might well think that I should examine you as to every check in this pile. However, I have looked at each check and hereby offer you a time-saving proposition. I am prepared to stipulate that every check written by you was drawn in good faith and for a current obligation, **IF** you will do me the courtesy—nay (I said 'nay'), the honor, of singing a few bars of your famous theme song, *Martha*."

Shocked silence was followed by Stern's anticipated explosion. He pounded the table, half-rose, and screamed at me, "You are making a travesty of this examination!!!" but his scream was truncated by Tracy's stern and unforgiving command.

"Sit down, Stern, and shut up."

Tracy turned to me and in his beautiful baritone of old said, "Bill, I am deeply flattered by your request." So saying, he turned full-face to the court reporter, tilted his head back just the right amount, and let loose.

"*Martha....RRRambling RRRose of the Wild Wood....*" He went on for a few more bars, then turned to me for approbation.

"Arthur," I said, "that was glorious. There's no other word for it."

"Thank you, Bill, thank you." Slight pause, then, "Are we through here?"

"Of course we are, Arthur," I replied. "I am most grateful to you."

"It was my pleasure, Bill, and a great pleasure indeed. Well," he said, rising from his chair and not even bothering to look at Stern, "I'm off to the Lambs Club. Ta ta, Bill. And say, you're from Washington, aren't you? Don't miss me Sunday night on the Kate Smith Show; nine o'clock on your Channel 5."

Tracy was gone like a puff of smoke. Stern grabbed the pile of checks, stuffed them in his briefcase without a word and without looking up, and hurried off.

I told the court reporter to be sure to triple the R's when she transcribed Tracy's rendition, and called my client to tell him that he had no case against Arthur Tracy. I added that I had won mine.

"A GOLDEN OLDIE"

This story has no relation whatsoever to Jason and the Golden Fleece, King Midas, Goldfinger, or the Treasure of the Sierra Madre. There are neither gods, magicians, spies, nor Mexicans involved. All we have is a series of out-of-the-ordinary events and human nature face to face with gold.

The wallet you can purchase today is substantially smaller in size than the wallet your grandfather and his grandfather lugged around, because from the founding of the Republic until the year 1933, American currency in all serious denominations came in large sized pieces of paper called gold certificates. Each of these pieces of paper certified that there had been deposited with the Treasurer of the United States a certain number of dollars—five dollars, ten dollars, twenty dollars, fifty dollars, one hundred dollars, one thousand dollars, even ten thousand dollars—in gold, and that the bearer of the certificate could drop around to the Treasury and pick up the gold any time he or she wanted to.

Ten thousand dollars was, and still is, a lot of money, and few people wanted such a sum lying in their safety deposit boxes or sitting around in their wallets when it could be drawing interest, so the big bills—the ten thousand dollar babies—were almost exclusively used by banks in transfer and settlement of accounts between them. To facilitate bank transfers, on March 14, 1900, Congress authorized the Secretary of the Treasury to vary the customary pattern of issuing gold certificates payable to *bearer*—that is, to whomever showed up with one—by issuing $10,000 certificates payable to *order*, that is, to a specific person or organization, who could then endorse it to someone else. In other words, the Secretary could print and issue gold certificates which were *checks*, just like the ones you write to your electric company. By statute, these "checks" were issued against gold coin deposited with the Treasurer of the United States, and, in the words of the statute, "the coin so deposited shall be retained in the Treasury and held for the payment of such certificates on demand, and used for no other purpose." The advantage of these "checks" was that they could only be transferred by authorized endorsement, so a thief could not cash one without committing the further crime of forging the required endorsement, and the party accepting one either knew his endorser or risked being out ten thousand bucks.

So these big babies, ten thousand dollar gold certificates printed by the Bureau of Engraving and Printing in Washington, carrying a picture of President Andrew Jackson, the words TEN THOU-SAND DOLLARS, the number 10,000, and the customary engraving, but showing blank lines for the insertion of the name of the payee, the date, and the ink signature of the authorized signatory, the Assistant Treasurer of the United States, on the obverse, but as blank as a clean sheet of typing paper on the reverse, circulated among the banks until 1933, when it became illegal for any and every American to own gold coin, gold bullion, or gold certificates.

Now: In their dealings with the United States Government from and after 1900, the banks often met their obligations with these gold certificates, and when the United States went off the gold standard, all gold certificates had to be turned in for Treasury certificates or Federal Reserve notes. Thus in 1933 and 1934 the Treasury Department accumulated vast stores of gold certificates, duly sorted them by denominations, and ultimately turned them over to the General Accounting Office.

One cold day in December of 1935, there was a major fire at the General Accounting Office in downtown Washington. Panicking in the smoke and flames, a clerk who had custody of the redeemed ten thousand dollar gold certificates payable to order grabbed the certificates on his desk, two hundred fifty of them, and threw them out of the window!

The following morning the Washington Post, the Washington Times, the Washington Herald, and the Washington Daily News all headlined the fire and excitedly reported that two and a half million dollars had been thrown out of a window. The newspapers reassured the reading public that the currency was unimpaired, because the Secretary of the Treasury had announced that all of the certificates had been recovered; all of them had been defaced by having been impaled on spindles leaving a large hole in each certificate; they were worthless; and should one turn up in spite of the foregoing, it should be immediately turned in to avoid prosecution. (As Ralph Waldo Emerson said, a foolish consistency is the hobgoblin of small minds.)

Fred Muntz was a little guy. He owned a cleaning and pressing shop in the suburbs, where he and his wife scratched out a living in calm and perseverance, and when he needed a lawyer, which was seldom, he called us. So to receive an excited telephone call from Fred was an unusual event, one that occurred in the Spring of 1957.

In a low, trembling voice, Fred first wanted to know who was on the line. "Who in the hell did you call?" Dad demanded. Fred persisted, so Dad finally said, "Billy and I and nobody else."

Fred said that it was critical that we drop whatever we were doing and come out to his house, right away! Dad insisted on knowing what the trouble was, but Fred said that he could not tell us over the telephone, but that it was urgent, whereupon he hung up.

Dad opined that Fred had finally shot Jenny, his ever-nagging wife, but that we had better go see, so we closed up shop and drove to Fred's house. It was mid-afternoon, but we could see from the street that every shade in the house had been drawn. Dad rang the doorbell, and a female voice inquired as to who was there. Dad gave me a look acknowledging that Jenny remained viable, and said, "Holmes and Watson." An overly excited male voice shouted, "Who is it?" "Wolf & Wolf," Dad answered equably.

Fred opened the door and we walked into darkness relieved

only by the dim light of a table lamp in the living room. "Throw the bolt, Jen," Fred ordered, and Jenny complied. Then Fred walked over to the table lamp, lifted it up, and with trembling fingers handed Dad an unsealed envelope. Dad, never lacking a sense of drama, opened the envelope very slowly and even more slowly withdrew the contents.

Gold certificate numbered M147607, in the denomination of ten thousand dollars and bearing the likeness of President Jackson, emerged in the half-light. It certified that $10,000 had been deposited with the Assistant Treasurer of the United States, and was payable in gold at his office, to the order of Federal Reserve Bank of N. Y. or Federal Reserve Agent at N. Y., New York. It was date-stamped AUG 3 1917 and, in addition to the engraved signatures of the Register of the Treasury and the Treasurer of the United States, bore an ink signature identified as Asst. Treasurer of U.S.

The reverse bore an unrestricted endorsement in blank, effectively making it a bearer instrument. It was pristine; nary a spindle had it encountered in its lifetime.

Fred asked us to take it along, determine its provenance (not his words), and ascertain its value. As we left, we saw the curtains coming up all over the house.

There are honest and helpful men and women working for our Government. It took less than a week for the Deputy Treasurer of the United States then serving to determine from the serial number that this certificate had been redeemed in an Federal Reserve interdistrict transaction on February 10, 1921, and that it had been regularly accounted for until December, 1935; he suggested that we telephone the Secret Service for further information.

We did so, and a very helpful Agent asked us to photocopy the certificate and bring the photocopy to his office; he explained that if we brought the certificate itself, the Secret Service was legally obligated to impound it. We did so, and that's when we heard the story of the December 1935 fire, the Treasury's announcement, and the aftermath, which was that certificates similar to Fred's had been turning up, a few each year, ever since 1935. What about the spindling, we asked. Poppycock, the Agent said; the report of full recovery being arrant nonsense, what harm a little more fabrication.

We asked the Agent if collectors could legally retain these certificates; the answer was negative. The Agent invited us to contact dealers to see for ourselves that no dealer would touch them. We did so, and he was right.

Ever so often, when we went to our vault we took out this big, beautiful, worthless piece of paper and fondled it, just as Fred must have after he bought it (although he would never tell us how he came into possession of it). Then one day Fred called to say that he had sold his shop and that he and Jen were moving to Florida, so would we please bill him for our time and mail the certificate to him by registered mail?

"No charge, Fred; it's been too much fun looking into it," said Dad, "but your check will be in the mail—registered." As it was, the following morning.

"THE GUNS OF BRODSKY"

Brodsky v. United States had to be filed in a great hurry. I took the requisite number of copies of the summons, the complaint, and the motions to the United States Courthouse and presented them to the Clerk, who stamped each cover sheet three times. First he stamped each sheet "Filed" with the date underneath. Then he stamped each sheet with the civil action file number. Lastly he rummaged among his rubber stamps and then applied the only one I fervently hoped not to see:

HOLTZOFF, J.
Goodbye, *Brodsky v. United States.*

Alexander Holtzoff, United States District Judge, was the first Federal judge before whom I had ever appeared. He was a legend. Short of stature and shorter of temper, he had co-authored one of the leading treatises on Federal practice. Having in some respects *written the book*, he judged *by the book* and invariably *threw the book* at everyone appearing before him, parties and lawyers alike, who expressed ideas differing in any way from his own 19th Century notions of proper conduct. His intellect was greatly respected; his rulings were often reversed by the Court of Appeals, on which sat a humanitarian or two.

My first appearance before Judge Holtzoff came about as a result of my hunger for trial practice. At the time I came to the bar our practice was predominately administrative, with a paucity of courtroom litigation, so I took advantage of the opportunity then offered to gain trial experience by volunteering to represent a criminal defendant without charge, in a program which provided a *quid pro quo* in the form of a follow-up assignment as counsel to a non-responding and therefore non-contesting spouse in a divorce case, with a fee of fifty dollars as bait.

My name came up on the list, and I was assigned the representation of Tyrone, age 17, who was charged with felonious assault. Tyrone, the United States alleged, had lain in wait outside a grocery store in a bad neighborhood in which lived a fine church-going lady. When the fine lady came out of the store carrying her groceries, with her purse suspended from a shoulder strap, Tyrone had rushed at the lady, seized the shoulder strap, and given a larcenous yank. This left the purse in the hands of Tyrone, the groceries strewn all over the sidewalk, and the lady lying in the street with a broken arm. Things being in certain respects clubby in that neighborhood, the lady knew exactly who had attacked her. Tyrone was arrested around the corner at his girlfriend's house by Officer Williams, the omnipresent cop on the beat, while the lady was en route to the hospital in the ambulance. The purse was nowhere to be found.

I interviewed Tyrone at the D. C. Jail. He denied any connection with the crime, telling me that he had been in bed with his girlfriend at her house for a solid week until Officer Williams appeared with a no-nonsense look in his eye and a pair of handcuffs in hand, both of which Tyrone knew from experience.

Tyrone dealt with me pleasantly but firmly. "This your first case?" he asked. Well, my first criminal case, I allowed.

"You got to investigate," instructed Tyrone. "Let me know if anybody but the old lady says they made me."

I looked blank.

"That means, made a positive ID of me," explained Tyrone patiently. "Get a witness list from the prosecutor—they got to give you that—and go talk to them." Effortlessly assuming the role of Tyrone's "junior," as the British barristers say, I asked Tyrone, "Where are we going with this?"

"They're trying me as an adult. They got two witnesses, I'm in deep shit; two-to-five, that's four years for sure, Baby. But I cop a plea to simple assault, just a misdemeanor, and I'm back in the slammer in time to play right field this Spring and hit the streets again come Fall."

"You've been there before?" I asked.

"Yeah. I just told you, I play right field."

So I got a list of witnesses and trooped some very mean streets interviewing them. To a man and woman they "made" Tyrone. When I tried the misdemeanor approach on the Assistant United States Attorney, he just laughed at me. At our conference in his office I made a mental note that his desk was piled high with case files; he was clearly much, much busier than I was. So I dropped into see him every week, playing the misdemeanor card each time and noticing each time that the piles on his desk were growing both larger and more numerous. By the third week we were on a first-name basis and his hair was coming down: "Get out of here, Bill; can't you see how busy I am?"

On the fifth visit I made the deal Tyrone wanted. The felonious assault charge was superseded by a charge of simple assault carrying a maximum sentence of one year, to which charge Tyrone entered a plea of guilty. On the appointed day the Assistant U. S. Attorney, Tyrone and I appeared in the United States District Court for the District of Columbia for sentencing. The presiding judge was Alexander Holtzoff.

The courtroom was crowded with the guilty and their lawyers. When the clerk called Tyrone's case, Tyrone was brought out of the cell block and delivered into a chair next to me at the defendant's table; the prosecutor sat at an adjoining table heaped with files. The clerk handed Tyrone's court file to Judge Holtzoff, who riffled through it and extracted three pages from the bottom of the file. He turned to, and on, the Assistant U. S. Attorney.

"Do I note correctly that this epitome of viciousness, charged with the crime of felonious assault against an elderly woman, is the subject of a reduction of charge to simple assault?"

The AUSA stood up, looked several feet away from Judge Holtzoff, and mumbled, "Yes, your Honor."

"The original charge having been dropped, and the accused having pled guilty to the superseding charge, I have no choice but to accept the plea. *But let me tell you*," he roared presciently, "when the day comes that this city is not fit for decent people to inhabit, *it will be your fault.*"

Continuing to roar, Judge Holtzoff addressed Tyrone. "*Stand up.*"

Tyrone stood up. The judge looked down at the file to catch my name and said to me, rather civilly, "Do you have anything to say before I pass sentence, Mr. Wolf?"

I had had no courtroom experience, but I had seen a lot of movies.

"Yes, Your Honor, I do. I hope that in passing sentence, Your Honor will take into account the tender years of this youth and his potential for reformation. If I may, I suggest that the assurances which he is prepared to give the Court that he has learned his lesson and learned it well...."

"Mr. Wolf," the judge interrupted, "my courtroom is crowded and I do not have time to listen to such rubbish. You have not seen his record of prior arrests"—in those days defense counsel was not afforded the resources made available today—"but the hardened criminal standing next to you is hardly the person you are so absurdly describing.

"I sentence the defendant to the maximum prison term established by law for the offense to which he has entered his plea of guilty, which is one year. If the United States Attorney did the job for which the citizenry pays him, I would better serve the community by awarding the defendant the five-year sentence he deserves. Clerk, call the next case."

I walked back to the cell block with Tyrone to say goodbye. Tyrone was ecstatic. "Man, did he stick it to the 'pros'! Mr. Wolf, you did great; if I had any money left, I'd give it to you. Tell you what; I'm gonna send you all my friends. Some of them got money." I asked Tyrone please not to send me any of his friends, as I was then and there retiring from the practice of criminal law. The AUSA stuck with it, kept accepting plea bargains, and is now a Federal judge.

Judge Holtzoff and I met again in the matter of *DeCenzie v. Postmaster General.* Working out of a burlesque theater in Oakland, California, the aptly named DeCenzie had placed ads in a number of pulp magazines offering a collection of twelve photographs of amply endowed females to all who would send him two dollars. He was doing a moderate amount of business when the Postal Inspectors struck, suspending his privilege of utilizing the United States mails on the ground that he was using same for the distribution of obscene literature.

I examined the offending photographs. There wasn't a single bare breast or bottom in the bunch, and by today's standards each lady depicted would be welcomed into the Legion of Decency dressed as she was, but today's standards were not yesterday's, so I advised DeCenzie that the case would be a tough one, highly dependent upon which judge we drew. DeCenzie decided to take his chances in court. I filed a suit in Federal Court asking that the Postmaster General be enjoined to restore DeCenzie's privilege of receiving the United States mail.

The luck of the draw was terrible; the case was assigned to Judge Holtzoff. As the facts of the case were essentially limited to the twelve photographs, the Court rolled my motion for a temporary restraining order, a temporary injunction, and a permanent injunction into one expedited hearing, and off to Court I went. The case was called, the Department of Justice lawyer representing the Postmaster General and I took our places, and I waited for the customary judicial nod toward plaintiff's counsel. I waited, and waited, and waited.

Judge Holtzoff was examining the photographs. Interminably, one at a time, buxom stems to curvaceous sterns, in ominous silence. Because he had the twelve photographs spread out before him on the bench, I could see that he kept returning to one of them; finally, he picked that one up and held it in front of him. I could not see which photograph he had picked up, but I knew that it was #6, which captured one of the lovelies, knees spread, rapturously enjoying a seat upon a wooden stump about the height and perhaps half the diameter of a fire plug, and I knew what his problem was. Certainly it was not the deciding of the case—the case was long lost—but the necessity to cloak love and lust in the raiment of disgust.

Finally he spoke, not to call on me for oral argument—he would brook no argument of this case—but to render his verdict.

"I find each of the photographs in suit, and particularly that bearing the number six...."—here he let #6 flutter daintily from his fingers—"to be morally offensive and legally obscene. Rarely do I encounter conduct more reprehensible than that of this defendant...."—not only was DeCenzie the plaintiff, not the defendant, but the proceeding was civil, not criminal, so I hazarded a soft interruption: "The plaintiff, if the Court please." This brought the judge up short.

He cleared his throat. "Restraining order and injunctions denied." So ruling, he gathered up the twelve photographs, placed them in the file folder, rose, and left the bench to return to his chambers—carrying the file folder with him!

The attorney representing the P. G. and I dared not look at each other until we had left the courtroom. Once in the corridor we were laughing so hard that a Marshal came out of another courtroom and told us to knock it off. We had seen each other for the first time an hour earlier and had never spoken a word to one another, but we went off together to an uproarious lunch.

Which brings me to "The Guns of Brodsky."

But first, a brief lesson in the history of military technology. For numerous millennia, the earliest of our forebears resolved their differences of opinion by throwing rocks at one another, often lethally. Then one historic day a rock-thrower who was balancing his flint rock in his hand preparatory to hurling it was surprised by an enemy rock which struck his, smashed a few fingers, and shattered his rock before he could throw it. Dancing in pain (and in bare feet), he stepped on a shard of what had been his rock and gave out an antediluvian howl—the shard had nearly sliced off a toe. When his several bleedings slowed to a trickle, he picked up the shard that had cut his toe, took it back to his cave, lashed it to a freshly cut sapling with mastodon sinew, and thereby invented the spear. Within the space of a few thousand years spear-hurling had superseded rock-throwing nearly everywhere. Then along came ever more sophisticated forms of knifery, each superseding the last, until single-shot gunfire rendered the sharp edge obsolete.

The repeating rifle quickly drove the musket from the field and survives to this day, but woe to the rifleman who has to face a foe armed with automatic riflery, and woe to the submachine gunner up against leadthrowers faster than his device.

BUT, dear reader, remember this: Each obsolete weapon has remained lethal and can find a market among those groups whose lack of technological sophistication and/or economic resources precludes their development or purchase of the very latest in killing machines. Even the rock is still in vogue, as the *intifada* in the Gaza Strip and on the West Bank of the Jordan River attests.

Brodsky was a wheeler-dealer who made his living making deals where he found them. He often found them in the eternal need of governments, national, regional and local, to upgrade whatever tools and techniques they have in hand. Want to convert your municipal transit system from streetcars to buses? Brodsky couldn't manufacture buses, but he could sell your streetcars to a city in Albania or Lower Volga or wherever. Need to dispose of your out-of-fashion army cots? Brodsky knew just which African army was in desperate need of cots. Brodsky was not without competition in the world of military disposition of yesterday's equipment, but he made his share of the deals that became available. He was an avid reader of the publications which carried Invitations to Bid, which was the customary route governmental organizations took in attempting to get the best prices for their discards.

One morning in the late 1960's Brodsky was browsing the Government's Invitations when he came across one of a character he had never seen before. Under the rubric "Scrap Metal" the Chief of Ordnance of the United States Army was soliciting bids for the privilege of coming onto the Anniston Arms Depot in Anniston, Alabama, not fifty miles from Brodsky's home base, setting up a machine shop, and, in strict accordance with the Corps of Ordnance Manual composed for this Invitation, rendering seventeen thousand Thompson submachine guns into scrap metal and carting the scrap metal away, all within the space of thirty days.

Brodsky was certain that this Invitation to Bid was a teaser; the Chief of Ordnance knew as well as he did that the cost of destroying 17,000 tommyguns and hauling away the resultant scrap metal would undoubtedly exceed the net proceeds of a subsequent sale of the scrap. Brodsky did a careful computation, thereby determining to his satisfaction that to rent eight metal saws and staff them with competent machinists for one month would cost about forty thousand dollars; that to hire common labor to stack and pack the scrap metal would cost another ten thousand dollars; that to haul the scrap to a warehouse and store it for six months pending resale would cost another ten thousand dollars; and that the most that could be realized from the resale of about 275 tons of scrap metal was two hundred dollars a ton, give or take ten dollars, for a gross of perhaps fifty-five thousand dollars and a net loss. So it was clear to Brodsky that the Chief of Ordnance expected that no bids would be submitted, thereby freeing him to dispose of the obsolete guns as he saw fit, free of Defense Department and Congressional accusation that he had not proceeded capitalistically and economically.

But Brodsky had an idea, one worth spending some time on, he told me. He drove to the Anniston Arms Depot, went to the Contracting Office, and asked for and received a copy of the freshly minted Corps of Ordnance Manual setting out the precise and incontrovertible requirements established by the Corps for the conversion of the Thompson submachine gun into scrap metal. Aha! The Manual specified that each tommygun be sawed through at two locations on an angle varying exactly thirty degrees from the vertical. The prescribed locations of the gun cuts were across the barrel, twelve inches from the muzzle, and through the receiver, one inch in front of the trigger. So cut, the Corps of Ordnance had determined, the most skillful gunsmith in the world could not piece together the three pieces of metal thereby generated into an operable submachine gun at less than ten times the cost of building such a gun from scratch.

Brodsky told me that this Invitation to Bid had given him his idea, one which he was certain had never occurred to the Chief of Ordnance and would not occur to anyone else. His basic cost would be in accordance with his calculations, and his idea would entail a further investment of maybe a hundred thousand dollars, but man oh man what a profit potential there was. Of the ten or twelve million Americans who had been under arms in World War II, there must be at least half a million who had blazed away at the enemy with a tommygun. If just three percent of these retired gunners could be tempted to buy an unbelievably unique souvenir to hang over their mantles, then Brodsky saw the opportunity to sell them such a souvenir, looking exactly like the tommygun of memory because it *was* the tommygun of memory, restored in every respect save operability and available from Brodsky Enterprises for six hundred dollars, while they last! Six hundred dollars times seventeen thousand guns equalled just over **ten million dollars!**

Brodsky submitted his bid, offering to pay the Government the sum of $2,000 in cash for the privilege described in the Invitation to Bid, and accompanying the bid with a performance bond and the required certifications as to his loyalty and integrity, neither of which bore the slightest blemish. He was the only bidder; his bid was perforce accepted.

Brodsky arrived at the Depot on the appointed day with his rented metal saws, his hired machinists, his packing crates and common labor, and his trucks on call. The Commanding Officer welcomed him graciously—this was the Deep South—opined that he would lose his shirt, admitted him into a large corral ringed with barbed wire wherein lay 17,000 neatly stacked tommyguns, and introduced him to the officer who would oversee the cutting operation to make certain that it complied with the Manual. Brodsky bade his team get right to work; with but thirty days in which to scrap 17,000 guns, he had no time to waste.

On the fourth day of the thirty allowed, Brodsky and his workmen arrived at the corral to find it secured against entry by a detail of six soldiers armed with the tommygun's successor. The sergeant in charge of the detail politely requested that Mr. Brodsky report to the office of the Commanding Officer for an explanation of his debarment from the corral. Brodsky rushed to this destination, where the Commanding Officer insisted that he sit down and have a cup of coffee. Brodsky, haunted by thoughts of ten million dollars taking wings and flying away from him, did not want to sit down or to have a cup of coffee, but he did as requested. The Commanding Officer, greatly discomfited, said that he had something most embarrassing to the Corps to tell Brodsky, which was this: The Manual prescribing the required procedure for the destruction of the Thompson submachine gun, carefully written by the Corps of Ordnance specifically for the bid which Brodsky had won, had come into the hands of the Bureau of Alcohol, Tobacco, and Firearms of the U. S. Treasury Department, which had jurisdiction over the manufacture, sale, distribution and possession of automatic weaponry pursuant to longstanding Act of Congress. ATF had engaged a journeyman machinist and stationed him at a metal saw set up in the practice gunnery range at the Marine Corps base at Quantico, Virginia. It had directed him to cut a tommygun exactly as prescribed by the Ordnance Manual, which he proceeded to do. It then instructed a journeyman welder to join the machinist at the sawing table. With stopwatch in hand, the presiding ATF official commanded "GO!" Fifty-five minutes later the machinist rammed a fifty-cartridge drum into place on their reconstruction, turned toward the target lane, and blasted an outlined enemy into oblivion. Estimated cost of reconstruction: Fifty dollars, declining with experience.

It was not that the Corps suspected Brodsky of having any

such design in store for the scrap metal he was creating, said the Commanding Officer, but the existence of such a possibility at such a low cost, coupled with the threat conveyed by the Director of the Bureau to the Chief of Ordnance to go straight to Congress, left Ordnance with no choice but to cancel Brodsky's contract and bring in the bulldozers to do the job of destruction the old-fashioned way. The Commanding Officer told Brodsky that the Chief of Ordnance had asked him to convey his personal regrets for the cancellation, which was in no way Brodsky's fault, and to offer Brodsky ten thousand dollars in compensation for his expenses to date.

Brodsky, with the roar of bulldozers destroying ten million dollars ringing in his mind's ear, caught the next plane to Washington and rushed to the office of Senator John Sparkman, where he was well and favorably known. He told the whole story to Senator Sparkman's administrative assistant, who immediately telephoned the Pentagon on Brodsky's behalf. Brodsky had to wait about an hour for telephone calls back and forth to be completed, after which the A.A. told him that true or false, the Treasury Department's report had stopped the Army in its tracks. Ordnance's offer of ten thousand dollars could be raised to fifteen, said the A.A., but if Brodsky wanted to try to stop the bulldozers and resume his work, the only possibility lay with judicial interposition. In other words, said the A.A., file a lawsuit, fast.

Brodsky arrived in our office in mid-afternoon. After he told us his story, I instructed my faithful secretary to cancel her plans for the evening, and I suggested that Brodsky check into a hotel, get a good night's rest, and reappear at our office at seven o'clock the next morning. Marian went out for sandwiches for herself and me while I started dictating into my Dictaphone; upon her return, she began to type while I continued to dictate. By two o'clock in the morning we had produced a summons and complaint, a detailed affidavit ready for Brodsky's signature, a motion for a temporary restraining order with draft order, a motion for a preliminary injunction, a motion for a permanent injunction, and—just in case—a notice of appeal to the United States Court of Appeals and a motion for temporary relief from that Court. The thrust of the lawsuit was that the Army should be restrained from destroying the guns until impartial experts could be convened to test the destruction technique prescribed by the Corps of Ordnance and the alleged reconstruction claimed by the Bureau of Alcohol, Tobacco and Firearms, and advise the Court as to whether or not Brodsky should be permitted to resume performance of his contract.

We filed the lawsuit at nine o'clock and, as I knew would be the case, lost it at the District Court level immediately upon its assignment to Judge Holtzoff. The distinguished judge held a hearing forthwith upon the arrival at the Courthouse of a cadre of Defense Department lawyers—Defense did not wait for the Justice Department to jump into the fray—and, as was usual with him, ruled from the bench. He expressed horror at the thought that a citizen (one of his favorite words, encompassing the entirety of the great unwashed) would even contemplate undertaking a project which threatened the lives of hundreds, nay thousands, of his fellow citizens with being machinegunned out of existence. He expressed recognition that the Defense Department, acting through the Corps of Ordnance, had authorized the project in question with callous disregard for public safety. He complimented the Treasury Department for the expansion of its responsibilities from mere guardianship of the public purse to guardianship of the public welfare. He denied our motion for a temporary restraining order as well as our other motions, cast a look of overwhelming scorn at Brodsky, and left the bench.

I persuaded the Defense Department lawyers to join Brodsky and me in an elevator ride down to the Clerk's Office, where I filed our Notice of Appeal, and then up to the sixth floor, where sat the United States Court of Appeals. The Calendar Clerk set our appeal down for hearing at two o'clock, right after lunch.

At two o'clock we all trooped into the courtroom. A panel of three well-lunched judges listened to my short-form version of the facts, heard from a Defense Department lawyer, and retired to consider their verdict. We won! (Sort of.) The Court of Appeals reversed Judge Holtzoff (as it loved to do) as to the motion for a temporary restraining order, sustained him as to the other motions, and granted Brodsky a ten-day stay, thereby halting the bulldozers for that period of time. Court was adjourned, and Brodsky asked me *what* we had won. I explained that we had been given ten days in which to take the matter of the temporary and permanent injunctions to the Supreme Court of the United States on an emergency basis. "What are our chances there?" Brodsky asked. None and none, I assured him, but there was some personal satisfaction in getting Judge Holtzoff reversed, even slightly.

"If you've gotten me ten days, you've done better than you think," Brodsky said to me. "Send me a bill." He left the Courthouse in the direction of the Senate Office Building, where he relayed the day's events to Senator Sparkman's A.A. Early the following week the Defense Department sent Brodsky a check for $25,000 and Brodsky removed his equipment from the Anniston corral. "You win some, you lose some," he said to me over the telephone later that week when he told me the aftermath of our day in court. Out of curiosity, I asked him if he had seen any bulldozers when he cleared out of the Anniston Depot. No, he said, but he could hear their roar in his sleep.

Ten years later I found myself sitting at the bar at Windows on the World, the spectacular restaurant atop the World Trade Center in New York. My lady love had gotten tied up at her office, she told me over the telephone, leaving me at loose ends until she appeared for dinner. Thus my seat at the bar.

There was a man about my own age sitting several empty seats away, and over the second martini he and I began to chat. When he disclosed that he was a lawyer from Alabama, I told him that I had once had an interesting case emanating from his home state involving, of all things, seventeen thousand tommyguns.

"Brodsky," he said. "When Brodsky called me that morning, I told him to catch the next plane to Washington."

I was without speech.

"Want to know where those guns are now?" he asked me.

"*Are?*" I asked incredulously.

"Are," he emphasized.

"They were bulldozed," I said.

"They're in Pakistan," he said. "The whole kit and caboodle."

"Was Brodsky in on the sale?" I asked.

"No way," he replied. Just then, his lady appeared. He shook my hand most formally, and away they went.

There's more.

In the month of June, in the year 1938, I successfully completed the sixth grade and ceremonially graduated from John Eaton School, P. S. 160, situated in the Cleveland Park section of Washington, D. C. I remained fond of John Eaton School ("Eaton, Eaton, Can't Be Beaten") over the years; not only had I had a fine time at John Eaton, but I was a legacy, my father having been schooled there in the nineteen teens. I therefore responded positively when one day in 1982 the mail brought an announcement that the John Eaton Class of '38 was holding its First and Forty-Fourth Reunion at the Tilden Street home of a classmate who had become a distinguished physician.

In attendance at the Reunion were two classmates I had kept up with, four or five more I recognized, perhaps a dozen I had no recollection of....and our most famous classmate, Sam Cummings. Sam Cummings had gone on to college, to Europe where he then lived, and to fame and fortune as the world's best known and most successful arms dealer. His enterprise, Interarmco, had been the subject of numerous newspaper and magazine articles over the years, and one evening I had watched a PBS hour entitled, of course, "Merchants of Death," which was mostly about Sam.

Sam and I had been friends at school, so we gravitated toward each other at the Reunion. After we had chatted about this and that, I told Sam that I had a pretty good story to tell him, one that had a surprise ending. I told him about *Brodsky v. United States*, and about my encounter at the bar at Windows on the World.

You can guess the rest.

"Want to know where those guns are now?" Sam asked me.

"Not Pakistan?" I asked back.

"Poland," Sam said. "But they're for sale; Poland is updating."

"How in the world do you know that?"

"That's my business, Bill. I keep a few choice items in my warehouses in Alexandria, Virginia, and in Europe, but my principal stock in trade is the set of card files on which I keep very accurate track of the contents, acquisitions, and dispositions of every arsenal in the world. I followed those 17,000 Tommies into Anniston, out to Pakistan, and on to Poland."

"Brodsky dreamed in vain?" I asked Sam.

"Seventeen thousand souvenirs?" Sam cocked an eyebrow at me and chuckled. "Yes, *whatever* Brodsky dreamed, he dreamed in vain."

I have no idea who bought the guns from the Poles, but this morning's newspaper carried the details of hideous slaughter in the small, backward country of Rwanda, landlocked in Central Africa. Hmmmm......

"THE ROAD TO GLORY"

Introduction

This is a drama about a drama; the lawyering comes at the end. As I'm going to present it to you in three highly complicated acts, I had better start with the *dramatis personae*.

Act I

Locale — Hollywood, California

The Backgrounders

William Fox   Billy Fox was one of the early moviemakers, producing silent films and exhibiting them in his chain of theaters throughout the country. (When I was a kid, when we wanted to see a first-run film, we went downtown, usually to "the Fox.") A losing legal battle with Thomas A. Edison and the Great Depression caused him to sell Fox Film Corporation to Joe Schenck (and, behind the scenes, L. B. Mayer) in 1935.

Louis B. Mayer   The mogul of moguls, his was the dominant ego on the Hollywood scene. He controlled every move and movie made by Metro-Goldwyn-Mayer, and was a secret partner of Joe Schenck's in the creation of Twentieth Century Pictures and its acquisition of Fox Film Corporation in 1935.

Joseph Schenck With his own money and L. B. Mayer's, Joe Schenck and his brother Nick founded Twentieth Century Pictures in 1933. When he acquired Billy Fox's company in 1935, he merged the two entities into Twentieth Century Fox Film Corporation. With his backing, Zanuck's genius made Twentieth Century Fox a giant in the film industry.

The Moviemakers

Darryl F. Zanuck

Born in Nebraska in 1902, Zanuck enlisted in the Nebraska National Guard at the age of fifteen, served with General Pershing in the punitive expedition into Mexico, fought in France in 1917, and at the age of twenty-one went to Hollywood, where he began as a laborer, clerked at a drugstore, then became a screenwriter, a studio manager, and an executive. By 1931 he was in charge of production at Warner Brothers; Joe Schenck (and L. B. Mayer) lured him away as a co-founder of Twentieth Century Pictures. With brief interruptions for service as a Colonel in World War II and as an independent producer in the early 60's, he ran Twentieth Century Fox from 1935 until 1971. The list of films he wrote, co-wrote, or produced runs into the hundreds; *How Green was My Valley, Gentleman's Agreement,* and *All About Eve* won Oscars.

Nunnally Johnson

A veteran screenwriter at Paramount, Johnson was tapped by Darryl Zanuck to help him run Twentieth Century Fox. His title was Associate Producer, but he always remained a writer at heart. His masterpiece was the script for *The Grapes of Wrath*, Twentieth Century Fox's biggest hit of 1940.

Howard Hawks

His honorary Oscar, awarded in 1974, says it all: "A master American filmmaker whose creative ef forts hold a distinguished place in world cinema." A graduate of Phillips Exeter Academy and Cornell University, he worked in the prop department of Famous Players-Lasky over summer vacations and went into the movie business in 1922. Billy Fox hired him as a director in 1925. In his 50 working years he directed *Scarface, Sergeant* York, Bringing Up Baby, His Girl Friday, To Have and Have Not, The Big Sleep, *Rio Bravo*, and dozens of other films, and provided dialogue for *Gone With the Wind* and *Gunga Din*. He was William Faulkner's Hollywood drinking buddy and patron saint.

The Screenwriters

Stephen M. Avery

A veteran "idea man" in Zanuck's stable of writers, he got a key component of the plot of *The Road to Glory* from a story told to him by a friend, director Charles Vidor, and passed it on to

Nunnally Johnson. After an enormous amount of negotiation, Zanuck "bought" the rights to this idea from Vidor and his partner, Leon Gordon.

The Ferrises

Veteran finishers of other people's scripts, they were in Zanuck's stable of screenwriters to provide "touches."

Joel Sayre

When he was 18, Sayre invaded Russia with the Canadian Expeditionary Force, spending seven months in Vladivastok.

After one term at Williams College, he enrolled at Oxford, graduating with a degree in English literature. While a reporter on the New York Herald Tribune, he wrote several well-received novels and began writing for the New Yorker. Then he went to Hollywood and joined Zanuck's stable. When World War II began, he returned to the New Yorker as a foreign correspondent. After the War he wrote for the New Yorker, Holiday, Life, and the Saturday Evening Post, and taught at the University of Pennsylvania.

William Faulkner

America has produced many fine novelists in the 20th century, but the "Big Three" have to be Faulkner, Fitzgerald, and Hemingway. They all drank a lot; Faulkner and Hemingway won the Nobel Prize.

The Players

Warner Baxter Virtually forgotten today, Baxter was the top money-making actor in Hollywood in 1936. He won his Oscar in 1929 as the star of Paramount's first sound film, *In Old Arizona.* His contract for *The Road to Glory* guaranteed that no actor's name would appear above his on the film or in advertising or publicity for it, but Zanuck talked him into letting the studio promote its new leading man, Fredric March, by giving March top billing. The rest is history.

Lionel Barrymore

The oldest and longest-lasting of the famous Barrymores, he began acting in films in 1910, won the Oscar in 1931, portrayed Dr. Gillespie in all 15 of the Dr. Kildare films, and amassed screen credits in nearly 300 movies.

Fredric March After service as an artillery lieutenant in World War I, March went on the Broadway stage. In 1928 he signed with Paramount to make "talkies"; when the contract expired in 1933, he began to freelance in films and on Broadway. He became a great star in both venues. He was nominated for the Oscar five times, and won twice.

Act II

Locale — Jackson, Tennessee

The Playwright

Robert H. Sheets

> Dropping out of high school to work in a novelty store, he aspired to literary glory—any way he could get it.

The Sponsors

Clarence Pigford

> Publisher of *The Jackson Sun*, owner of radio station WTJS, senior partner of the law firm of Pigford & Key, American Legionnaire, and Big Man in Jackson.

Albert Stone Pigford's right hand man, and thus also a Big Man in Jackson.

Legionnaires Led by Pigford and Stone, the John A. Deaver American Legion Post No. 12 financed the production of Sheets' play *The Road to Glory* at Jackson High School and at Bells High School.

Mrs. Merwin The high school drama coach who directed both performances of Sheets' play.

The Players

William Miller
Charles Miller College boys enrolled at Lambuth College in Jackson from September 1934 until June 1936. They owned a certain typewriter and performed in Sheets' play.

Roy Hardcastle
>   A large college football player whose nickname was
>   "Ox" and a performer in Sheets' play.

Townspeople   The rest of the cast of Sheets' play.

Act III

Locale — Washington, D. C.

The Judge

James W. Morris   United States Federal Judge.

The Lawyers

William B. Wolf
Fulton M. Brylawski
Simon Fleishman   Washington lawyers who kept offices
>   together in a loose association which lasted
>   for thirty years. They were the trial team
>   for Twentieth Century Fox Film
>   Corporation.

H. L. McCormick
& Horace Lohnes   Washington lawyers in the firm of
>   DowLohnes, which had represented
>   Pigford in obtaining the license for radio
>   station WTJS, and to which Pigford sent
>   Sheets to bring his lawsuit against
>   Twentieth Century Fox.

The Plaintiff

Robert H. Sheets

The Defendant

Twentieth Century Fox Film Corporation

The Witnesses

For the Plaintiff   Robert H. Sheets
                           William Miller
                           Charles Miller
                           C. C. Miller
                           Mrs. C. C. Miller
                           Mrs. Merwin
                           Roy Hardcastle
                           Townspeople
                           Typewriter Expert

For the Defendant
By Deposition   Darryl Zanuck
                           Nunnally Johnson
                           Howard Hawks
                           William Faulkner
                           Joel Sayre
                           Stephen M. Avery
                           Walter Ferris
                           Violet Kemble-Cooper Ferris
                           Mail Room Personnel
                           The Postmaster, Jackson, Tennessee

In Court   William Faulkner
                           Joel Sayre
                           Jack Bechdolt
                           Rev. Frank Stickney

Virgil Stickney
Richard E. Seeburger
Plymouth Dealer
Pinkerton Man
Typewriter Expert

Epilogue

United States Department of Justice
Federal Bureau of Investigation
The Imperial Japanese Fleet

* * * * * * * * *

The Road to Glory was a blockbuster motion picture released by Twentieth Century Fox Film Corporation in the late summer of 1936. The screenwriting credits went to William Faulkner—yes, *the* William Faulkner—and Joel Sayre; the executive producers were Darryl Zanuck and Nunnally Johnson; the director was the renowned Howard Hawks; and the principal actors were Fredric March, Lionel Barrymore, and the now virtually forgotten winner of the 1929 Oscar for Best Actor and in 1936 the highest-paid actor in Hollywood, Warner Baxter.

Twentieth Century Fox Film Corporation (hereinafter "Fox," as we lawyers say) had been spawned in 1935 by the marriage of Fox Film Corporation to Twentieth Century Pictures, Inc. Zanuck had been lured from Warner Brothers to Twentieth Century Pictures by its founder, Joe Schenck, two years before the merger; Zanuck brought in Johnson, a prominent screenwriter with production experience. Hawks had become famous as a director of silent films for Fox Film Corporation; he slid smoothly into directing "talkies," remaining in the top rank of directors until his death in 1977.

One of the first novels published after the Armistice ended

World War I on November 11, 1918, was Roland Dorgeles' "Les Croix de Bois," published in Paris on April 14, 1919. Literally translated into English as "Wooden Crosses," the novel was published in London by Heineman & Company on Armistice Day, 1920, and in New York by G. P. Putnam's Sons the following February.

On March 17, 1932, *Les Croix de Bois* came to the screen at the Moulin Rouge Theatre in Paris. Produced by Pathé-Natan Studios, the film, following Dorgeles' story line, incorporated breathtaking battle footage shot by French Army photographers, a number of whom were killed in the effort, and realistically staged combat scenes.

Les Croix de Bois was never released in the United States, but its existence and contents were of course known in Hollywood. Anxious to get the merger of Twentieth Century Pictures and Fox Film off to a flying start, Zanuck, who had fought in both General Pershing's Mexican campaign and with the A.E.F. "somewhere in France," bought the rights to *Les Croix de Bois* from Pathé-Natan in order to make use of its battle scenes, although he had not decided *how* he was going to use them; he had no interest in using Dorgeles' story line.

Zanuck put the question of how best to use these battle scenes to Johnson and Hawks. Johnson took direct control of the project. Turning to Fox's stable of screenwriters—each studio's assembly of writers under contract was called a stable, never a gaggle or a covey of screenwriters—he charged screenwriter Stephen Morehouse Avery with the responsibility of suggesting an appropriate "treatment," the first step in the production of a filmable script. Avery viewed the battle scenes and, using the title *Wooden Crosses*, wrote Johnson a set of notes suggesting characters and a possible plot for a film incorporating the war footage.

Johnson and Zanuck reviewed Avery's notes and turned them over to Joel Sayre, a well-known writer then in Fox's stable, for the development of a story line which could be scripted and filmed. Sayre, working with Johnson and Zanuck, produced an outline which inspired Zanuck to decide that the nascent movie deserved and required very serious treatment.

By 1935 William Faulkner had plenty of fame but very little money. Howard Hawks, who knew Faulkner well, greatly admired his writing, and came to his financial rescue time after time, persuaded Zanuck that his good friend and huntin'-fishin'-and-drinkin' buddy Faulkner should be engaged to work with Sayre in the conversion of Sayre's outline into a script. Faulkner promptly came to Hollywood. He, Sayre, and Zanuck developed a so-called "rough script" dated December 31, 1935—dates, good reader, are very important in this story—which contained full dialogue and directions for the actors. Numerous story conferences followed, Faulkner and Sayre working with Zanuck, Johnson and Hawks. A more polished script emerged on January 14, 1936, and a "shooting script," still bearing the title *Wooden Crosses*, was printed a week later.

The shooting script was then handed to stablemates Walter Ferris and Violet Kemble-Cooper Ferris for final polishing. This husband-and-wife team made certain revisions which, as was the Hollywood custom, were dated, printed on blue paper, and inserted into the shooting script. The last blue page inserted was dated February 3, 1936.

Zanuck and Johnson decided that the title *Wooden Crosses* was overly downbeat and tentatively changed it to *Zero Hour*. Hawks had a better idea. In 1926 he had directed a silent film for Fox Film Corporation entitled *The Road to Glory*. He suggested to Zanuck that as Fox had acquired the rights to that title in the merger and thus would not incur any acquisition cost, *Zero Hour* be rechristened *The Road to Glory*. And so it was.

Zanuck and Johnson cast the film with Fox's three best-known contract actors, Warner Baxter, Fredric March, and Lionel Barrymore, and an ingenue, June Lang, and Hawks shot the film in February and March, 1936, making slight changes in the dialogue (but not noting them on the shooting script) as he went along.

So-called "movie magazines" were extremely popular in the 1930's. The most widely circulated and read was Silver Screen, long a staple on newsstands and in beauty salons. It was the Hollywood habit for every major studio to send the shooting script of an important and soon-to-be-released film to Silver Screen in the hope that the magazine would publish a feature article reproducing substantial segments of the script as a "teaser." As soon as *The Road to Glory* was "in the can," as the saying went, the Fox publicity department sent the retitled shooting script to Silver Screen and Silver Screen assigned staffer Jack Bechdolt to write a major piece about it. Bechdolt did as instructed, reproducing large segments of the shooting script linked by description and a few lines of supposed dialogue which Bechdolt invented to suggest more romance than was actually in the script; his article appeared in the July issue of the magazine, which was published on June 5, 1936, some three months before the film was released throughout the United States. Courtesy of Fox's publicity department's other efforts, blurbs touting the impending release of *a multi-million-dollar epic of the Great War entitled "The Road to Glory" and featuring genuine battle scenes filmed by courageous French military photographers, starring Warner Baxter, Fredric March and Lionel Barrymore* had already appeared in the trade press.

The good citizens of Jackson, Tennessee, seventy-five miles or so northeast of Memphis, were by and large oblivious of the much-ballyhooed release until the film came to town in November of 1936. However, one Jacksonian was very much aware of the existence and impending release of *The Road to Glory*. This citizen, a youth but twenty-one years old, had made a habit of going to the public library once a week to read *Variety, Billboard,* and *Film Daily* in search of new ideas—other people's new ideas—for scripts, because scripts had already made him locally famous. His name was Robert H. Sheets.

The real reason Bob Sheets had dropped out of Jackson High School in the Spring of 1932 was that his mother desperately needed the money he earned at the novelty store to feed her family. Her other son Jimmy's conviction that he was a great musician wasn't even worth the occasional ten dollar bill he got for a weekend gig, so either Bob worked or the Sheets family starved. But that wasn't Bob's story.

Bob would have been a great public relations man. In fact, Bob *was* a great public relations man for his one and only client: Bob Sheets. In no time at all, his former classmates were telling each other exactly what Bob so carefully inspired, which was that Bob Sheets, the star of every English Composition class he had ever enrolled in, had left Jackson High because it had nothing left to offer him; he was writing at home, night after night, and when he was ready, Watch Out, World! Bob Sheets was going to put himself and Jackson, Tennessee, on the map, just like William Faulkner was doing not so far away in Mississippi. (Their worlds, his and Faulkner's, would collide....but that was later.)

Bob had a friend at the local daily newspaper, *The Jackson Sun*, and the friend knew that Bob was doing some important writing, so the friend was delighted for Bob but not totally surprised when Bob told him that he had some awfully good news that *The Sun* might be interested in publishing. Secretly, Bob said, secretly and without telling a soul, he had entered a scriptwriting contest sponsored by Warner Brothers, the movie people, and he had won! The script was entitled *Anne of Westmar Square* and Warner Brothers would probably make a movie out of it.

This was news in Jackson, Tennessee, and *The Sun* gave it a prominent place, trumpeting that a local boy just 18 years of age had accomplished a remarkable feat. Two days after the newspaper article was published, Bob sought out his friend and told him that he had forgotten to mention that *Anne* had won him a thousand dollar prize. *The Sun* published this fabulous news the following day.

There wasn't a shred of truth to Sheets' story. He had neither written a script nor won a prize, but what he *had* won was sudden and much-coveted prominence. People went out of their way to drop into the novelty store to chat with the newly famous and newly rich author. Was he working on another script? You bet your life! What was it about? It'll cost you 35 cents to find out, joked Bob, when the movie comes to town, and some of that 35 cents will be mine.

Then came the pressure. The adulation Bob had wrought bred impatience: Are you really writing another script? Admiration turned to skepticism, and Bob faced a reality. He had either to write something, really write something, or get laughed out of town.

One afternoon a friend dropped into the novelty store and handed Bob a manuscript. Bob took it home and read it. Entitled *Jeanne,* it was a story about a French girl named Jeanne and her patriotic adventures during the World War. The author was Mrs. Muse—*old* Mrs. Muse, not her daughter—and Bob, the literary expert, was asked his opinion of it. Pretty good, he said; I think I'd like to turn it into a play. Go right ahead, he was told; Mrs. Muse would like that.

So he did. Bob drafted a script, and when he was satisfied with it, he had two great ideas. One concerned the title. *Jeanne,* Bob thought, conveyed nothing, but a film title he remembered from the days of silent films, *The Road to Glory,* had a wonderful ring to it, so that became the title of the play. The other great idea concerned Clarence Pigford, who owned *The Jackson Sun,* and Albert Stone, Pigford's right hand man, both of whom were guiding spirits in the Jackson American Legion.

The Jackson Sun was founded in 1822 and remained under local ownership until 1973 when its owners, the Pigford family, sold it to the Cowles Organization, publisher of the Des Moines Register and Tribune, which continues to publish it today. In the 1930's the president of The Sun Publishing Company and the publisher of *The Sun* was Clarence E. Pigford; the executive vice president of Sun Publishing was Albert A. Stone, Sr., who worked for Pigford from 1919 until he retired when the newspaper was sold to Cowles. Pigford and Stone were very large fish in the small-town pond in which they swam, and of considerable importance throughout Tennessee. Both of them were extremely active in the

Jackson community. They (and thus *The Sun*) had an abiding interest in veterans' affairs. Stone had served in the Navy during the Great War; his obituary, published in *The Sun* on July 5, 1983, under a headline printed in type more than an inch high, related his continuing involvement in veterans' affairs in these words:

He was cited in 1968 by the American Legion as "State Man of the Year" and was recognized by local legionnaires for 50 years of service. He was a past commander of John A. Deaver American Legion Post No. 12, charter member and past commander of Cocks-Danuiels Veterans of Foreign Wars, Post No. 1848, and a member of the Madison County Barracks 1897, Veterans of World War I.

Mr. Stone chaired a Veterans' Day observance, "Bells Across the Nation," which won him national recognition, and received the VFW National Citizenship Award. He served as aide-de-camp to the VFW National Commander.

Upon Pigford's death his widow, Sally Person Pigford, succeeded him as president of Sun Publishing and as publisher of *The Sun*, and at her death in 1973, to quote her obituary, "Mrs. Pigford was very active in carrying on the work of completing the Memorial Carillon after her husband's death. The carillon, housed in First Presbyterian Church, is dedicated to veterans of World Wars I and II."

Pigford and Stone were entrepreneurs as well as newspapermen and civic boosters; in the early '30's, on behalf of Sun Publishing, they applied to and obtained a license from the Federal Communications Commission for radio station WTJS. Then as now, to become a licensee of the FCC required the services of legal counsel, usually a Washington law firm specializing in communications law. Pigford, who in addition to his many other activities was the senior partner of the law firm of Pigford & Key, had selected the Washington firm of Dow & Lohnes for this purpose, and it had rendered him good service.

In the 1920's and 1930's the American Legion was a potent political force throughout the United States. It remained so, particularly in small and medium-sized towns, by extensive community activity, sponsoring civic events, awarding good citizenship medals at high school graduations, and involving itself in innumerable aspects of daily life. Its leadership was usually the town leadership.

Bob Sheets asked his friend to show his new script to Pigford and Stone and to remind them that he was the young man who had won Warner Brothers' thousand dollar prize a few years earlier. Stone read and liked the script, loved the title, lauded it to Pigford, and American Legion sponsorship was thereby in the bag. Mrs. Merwin, the drama coach at Jackson High, was enlisted as director, and the town of Jackson was buzzing with the news that Bob Sheets was *allowing* his latest play to be staged with local talent *before* it became a motion picture. Mrs. Merwin cast "The Road to Glory" with several of her favorite graduates and it was produced on February 15, 1935, at Jackson High School, with half the town in attendance, and again the following weekend at Bells, a small town fifteen miles from Jackson. It was a smash hit, and its author (Mrs. Muse had slipped out of mind) was once again a celebrity. He was nineteen years old.

In November of 1936, Fox's *The Road to Glory* opened in Jackson. *The Road to Glory*? Never mind the differences between the story line of Sheets' play and the story line of the film; after all, you couldn't present an actual war on a high school stage. Friend after friend and acquaintance after acquaintance dropped into the novelty store to tell Sheets that Twentieth Century Fox had stolen his play. What was he going to do about it? Thanks to his reading habits, he was fully prepared for the question. I am going to sue them for a million dollars, he said. Which he did.

Clarence Pigford was not easily gulled. Before he committed himself and his colleagues to the financing of Sheets' lawsuit, he required Bob to come to his law office where he cross-examined him carefully as to details and dates. Based on Bob's responses to his questions, Pigford prepared eight affidavits which Bob duly obtained. The thrust of these affidavits was that in December of 1934 and January of 1935, Bob Sheets had first handwritten and then, borrowing the use of their Underwood Model No. 5, typed a motion picture scenario called "The Road to Glory" in the dormitory room of two of his friends, Bill and Bud Miller, brothers then attending Lambuth College in Jackson; that Sheets had rewritten the scenario to adapt it to the stage; that several of the affiants had performed in the play when it was produced in February of 1935; that Sheets had mailed the scenario to "Fox Pictures Corporation" that same month; that "Fox Pictures Corporation" had written him a letter, since lost, thanking him for his submission but stating that at present it could not use his scenario; and that the plot, characters, and dialogue shown on the screen were in substantial part identical with Sheets' scenario.

These affidavits fully satisfied Pigford. He opened the purse strings and sent Sheets to Washington to meet with Horace L. Lohnes and H. L. McCormick at the offices of Dow & Lohnes. Sheets provided Lohnes and McCormick with his story and his scenario. Not having available a copy of the script of the motion picture, they ingeniously sent a secretary with shorthand skills, nimble fingers, and a pack of steno books to attend the film, which was still showing in neighborhood theaters, as many times as she found necessary; in those days, a major film opened in one movie palace "downtown," ran as long as the crowds came, and then moved "uptown" into neighborhood theaters for several months. The mission of the secretary was to write down the dialogue as it was spoken; the purpose was to append to Sheets' initial court pleading both Bob's scenario and as faithful a copy as could be made of the script of the film.

Lohnes and McCormick filed Sheets' Bill of Complaint in the District Court of the United States for the District of Columbia (today called the United States District Court for the District of Columbia—but let's settle for Federal Court) on July 6, 1937; it was stamped In Equity No. 64876. The Bill of Complaint alleged that prior to February, 1935, Sheets had written an original manuscript which he had entitled "The Road to Glory"; that in February, 1935, he had submitted this manuscript to Twentieth Century Fox Film Corporation; and that shortly thereafter the manu-script had been returned to him, ostensibly rejected. The Bill fur-ther alleged that on or about November 15, 1936, Sheets learned that Twentieth Century Fox had made and was exhibiting a film entitled *The Road to Glory*; that at the first opportunity he had gone to see the film; and that he found that what Fox had pro-duced was his screenplay, wherefore he alleged "that said screen play or picture did and does constitute a pirating of the plaintiff's words, scenes, arrangements, dialogue, ideas....The copying, pi-rating and simulation of the language, scenes and settings are too numerous to mention in the body of this bill of complaint."

All Bob Sheets wanted was money damages, an accounting for all profits earned by the film, an injunction against further exhibi-tion of the film, and the turnover to him, or destruction under order of court, of all prints of the film. The Washington newspa-pers and the trade press picked up the filing of the Bill of Com-plaint and headlined Sheets' demands as "Million Dollar Law-suit."

A little genealogy is now in order. My forebears went into the movie business in Washington around 1908. In the 1920's they sold out to the Stanley Corporation of America, which became Stanley-Warner, which became Warner Brothers, but they contin-ued to maintain several presences in the business for a long time after selling out. Uncle Julian functioned as Warner Brothers' man-ager of area real estate for the next forty years or so; Uncle Fulton became and remained a preeminent copyright lawyer representing not only Warner Brothers but all of the major studios in their Washington work, sharing offices and trial work with my grandfa-ther, then my father, and later my father and me; and we always had passes to Warner Brothers theaters. Thus it was in the natural order of things that when the manager of Fox's local film exchange was visited by the United States Marshal and served with a sum-mons and Sheets' Bill of Complaint, the manager called Joe Schenck in New York, Schenck called Zanuck in Hollywood, Zanuck called Fox's lawyers in L. A., and Fox's lawyers called Uncle Fulton. The summons and Bill of Complaint were delivered to Uncle Fulton the following day. Uncle Fulton handed them to my father; thus began the memorable experience ever after known in our family as The Sheets Case.

Dad prepared an Answer to the Bill of Complaint denying all of Sheets' allegations adverse to the interests of Fox, Uncle Fulton sent Dad's draft to California counsel for review (in seven minutes, by ThermoFax!), and after quick California endorsement mailed a copy of the finished product to Sheets' lead counsel, H. L. McCormick, and filed the original in the Federal Court comfortably within the 20 days allotted for response. Then the real work began.

The defense team, augmented by Uncle Si, a quasi-relative and expert legal researcher, was well versed in the law of copyright; Uncle Fulton was a dean of the copyright bar and the author of numerous learned articles on the subject. The team knew that under the prevailing legal precedent (then and now), the law recognized that because a plaintiff alleging plagiarism can rarely if ever present eyewitness testimony that the defendant sat with the plaintiff's work in hand and physically copied it, circumstantial evidence would bring the plaintiff's allegations of plagiarism to issue if a preponderance of such evidence manifested that (1) the plaintiff's work product antedated the defendant's work product, (2) at the time(s) and place(s) that the defendant prepared his work product, he or she had access to the plaintiff's work product, and (3) the defendant's work product had substantial similarity to the plaintiff's work product. In lawyer's shorthand, a plaintiff alleging that his or her work has been plagiarized must prove *access* and *similarity* in order to present a court with the question to be adjudicated, which is, Did the defendant copy the plaintiff's work?

Thus the defense to a charge of plagiarism has many aspects. Defense counsel's threshold enterprise consists of fact-finding in the channels indicated by the requirements of proof that the law imposes on the plaintiff. The principal questions of fact to be explored at the outset are:

1. Who wrote the defendant's work?
2. When, where, and under what circumstances?
3. What persons will testify to those facts?
4. What reputations do those persons have for veracity (or lack thereof)?
5. Did the defendant—in a collective corporate enterprise, did the defendant's writers—have access to the plaintiff's work?
6. Are the two works similar, in whole or in meaningful part?
7. If so, is the similarity merely conceptual, or does a close comparison of the words and phrases suggest non-independent creation (in plain English, copying)?
8. When, where, and under what circumstances did the plaintiff write his or her work?
9. To what extent, and by what means, was the plaintiff's work published?
10. By what means does the plaintiff allege that the defendant gained access to his or her work?

For the purposes of the Sheets Case, Dad divided these questions and their components into two broad categories. One category consisted of those questions the answers to which would come from Fox's people; the other category consisted of those questions which would have to be answered by Sheets and his witnesses.

Dad reviewed his list of questions and his categorization of them with Uncle Fulton and Uncle Si and sent them off to California counsel accompanied by the request that they have Zanuck identify the producer(s), the director, and the screenwriter(s) who created "The Road to Glory" and direct those persons to make direct contact with Dad and give him their unqualified cooperation throughout the pendency and the trial of the lawsuit. Zanuck responded to this request by designating Nunnally Johnson as the "point man" to be certain that the defense team was provided with full cooperation and with any and all tools they might request.

Johnson and Dad then had a long conference by telephone, immediately following which a print of *The Road to Glory* was flown to the Washington office of Fox where Dad and the Uncles had their first (of dozens) professional viewing of the film. Johnson also had several copies of Fox's complete file of memoranda, scripts, fragments of dialogue, and correspondence flown to Dad, and he instructed the Fox publicity department to send Dad a copy of its entire file.

After Dad and Uncle Si had thoroughly reviewed Fox's files, they made new lists of questions which they then put to the persons whose roles were suggested by the film credits and revealed by the Fox files. The film credits listed the screenwriters as William Faulkner and Joel Sayre, but the outlines, memoranda, scripts, and signed notes of story conferences established that Avery, Zanuck, Johnson, Hawks, and the Ferrises all had a hand in creating the script. Each of them had to be thoroughly questioned as to the sources not only of their own ideas and contributions, but also as to the ideas and contributions put forth and made by the others.

Paragraph 5 of Sheets' Bill of Complaint alleged that Sheets had sent his script to Fox "on or about the month of February, 1935," and that "shortly after" Fox's receipt it had returned the script to him, writing him that Fox could not use it. To counter this allegation, Dad asked Johnson to have the appropriate Fox employees send him the then-prevailing instructions to mail room employees as to how they were to deal with unsolicited manuscripts. Uncle Fulton told Dad that all of the major studios had long since adopted and promulgated the protective policy of first logging in and then returning all material that came in "over the transom" to the sender unopened when a return address appeared on the enclosing envelope, and destroying, unopened, all unsolicited material received without a return address displayed. Dad asked Johnson to send him the Fox mail room logs for the months of December, 1934, through April, 1935, these months comfortably comprehending "on or about the month of February, 1935."

Dad and Uncle Si proceeded to interview all the contributors to the script of "The Road to Glory." The recollections of each collaborator were transcribed, converted into statements, and returned for correction, expansion, and signature.

This established the Twentieth Century Fox story. Dad had no doubt whatsoever that there had been plagiarism—the similarity of the scripts which Sheets' Bill of Complaint alleged and Dad's own comparisons confirmed could not possibly have resulted from coincidental composition. If his clients' people were telling the truth—which, Dad's experience at the Bar told him, was not always the case—then the plagiarist must be Sheets! But when, and where, and how? For the lawyers on both sides of the case, it was time to start taking depositions.

All in all, some forty witnesses were deposed, some in Washington, some in Hollywood and Los Angeles, some in St. Louis, and some in Jackson, Tennessee. Dad explored every aspect of Sheets' allegations; when Sheets testified that he had "probably" mailed his scenario to Fox by registered mail, Dad promptly subpoenaed and examined the Postmaster of Jackson, Tennessee, who could find no record of such a registration. McCormick, remembering the old saw about a camel being a horse that had been designed by a committee and scenting vulnerability, dug into the question of exactly who had written exactly which lines of the shooting script, a question that (depending on the witness) developed either a variety of conflicting answers or no answer at all. There was some comic relief in the deposition process. Dad came back from the deposition sessions in Jackson saying that the townspeople were so solidly behind Bob Sheets that not even the whores in the hotel lobby would speak to Uncle Si and him, and McCormick's examination of Nunnally Johnson was conducted in, not at, Johnson's swimming pool in Beverly Hills, Johnson dogpaddling while listening and responding to the questions and the court reporter sitting poolside in her swimsuit, steno machine on her lap and feet dangling in the water.

Early in the course of trial preparation Dad knew what Bob Sheets had done. He knew because he made a minutely detailed comparison of Sheets' scenario with the shooting script of the film and the embellishments which Jack Bechdolt had created in his piece in Silver Screen. Sheets had done a masterful job of creativity, changing names of characters and short speeches just enough to leave room for the impression that minor alterations had been what Fox's writers had made to his composition rather than the other way around, but he made one mistake that convinced Dad that Sheets, not Fox, was the plagiarist, and that was to doctor a little, but not much, some dramatic material that appeared neither in the shooting script nor in the film but that Bechdolt had invented for his article in Silver Screen.

If the truth were that Sheets had taken a copy of Silver Screen magazine and counterfeited his scenario from Bechdolt's article, then he could not have done this before the July 1936 edition of Silver Screen was published on June 5, 1936. But not only had Bob Sheets sworn under oath that he had first handwritten and then typed his scenario in the Miller brothers' room at Lambuth College in December of 1934 and January of 1935, but both Bill and Bud Miller swore that this was the truth. The testimony of Mrs. Merwin and the members of the cast of the play could be discounted because they testified about Bob Sheets' *script*, not his *scenario*, and Sheets disavowed any claim that his script had been plagiarized; his testimony was that both script and scenario came from thoughts he had had about the World War, but that the plots and dialogue were only related by the common theme of the Great War, and that he had never submitted the script of his play to Fox or anyone else.

The Miller brothers had been Sheets' friends, but they were not his intimates and they had little motive to lie on his behalf. Both of them were unshakable in testifying that when they entered Lambuth College in September of 1934, their father had given them the Underwood typewriter to take to school with them, and that they had it there throughout their two years at Lambuth College, before they transferred to Arkansas State in their junior year. Dad didn't believe it, but he did not know how to prove that their testimony was wrong.

As the depositions of the Fox producers, director, and screenwriters proceeded, Dad became more and more convinced that he would have to hit upon a way of refuting the Miller brothers' testimony, because the Fox witnesses' testimony as to the creation of the script of *The Road to Glory* became more and more contradictory and less and less comprehensible. When the lawsuit came to trial, Dad knew, the learned judge would want to know exactly who wrote exactly what parts of the film script, and to Dad's dismay neither Zanuck nor Johnson, nor Hawks nor Avery, nor Sayre nor the Ferrises, and least of all Faulkner, could give a straight answer to that question. Hopefully the judge would understand that film scripts pass through so many hands that the parentage of particular words becomes unascertainable, but this process constituted a monumental handicap in court. In short, as Dad saw it, defense in the form of a demonstrable claim of authorship by an author was impossible; he would have to prove that Sheets was a cheat and a liar and that the testimony of the Millers should not be believed.

McCormick mailed weekly reports to Clarence Pigford. They grow ever more optimistic as he reports the results of his depositions of Zanuck, Faulkner, Sayre, *et al.*; nobody knows who wrote what, he reports, and Sheets' affidavits have been fully supported by the testimony given by the affiants, unshaken by Wolf's cross-examinations. He adds that at the deposition of Sheets, by now a soldier in the United State Army, Bob stood up wonderfully under five days of blistering attack by Wolf.

The trial of *Sheets v. Twentieth Century Fox Film Corporation* began on November 8, 1939, in the United States District Courthouse in Washington, D. C., Mr. Justice James W. Morris presiding. Present in the courtroom were Judge Morris (who had served with the American Expeditionary Forces in France), his clerk, his bailiff, and his courtroom reporter; plaintiff Robert H. Sheets, on leave from his station as a private in the United States Army at March Field, California, for the duration of the trial; Messrs. H. L. McCormick and Horace L. Lohnes, for the plaintiff; Messrs. Fulton Brylawski, William B. Wolf, and Simon Fleishman, for the defendant; and members of the working press from the four Washington dailies, the New York Times, and Film Daily. Judge Morris instructed his clerk to call the pending matter, the clerk intoned "Robert H. Sheets versus Twentieth Century Fox Film Corporation, Equity Number 64,876," and Judge Morris nodded toward H. L. McCormick, who rose to express the traditional hope that his opening statement and proof of facts would please the court.

Sheets' lawsuit had been filed "In Equity." Because of the ancient distinction inherited from England between an action at law, which affords the litigants the right to trial by jury, and an action in equity, in which the facts as well as the law are determined by a judge sitting without a jury, *Sheets v. Twentieth Century Fox Film Corporation* imposed upon Judge Morris the responsibility of deciding whether a preponderance of the evidence satisfied him that Fox had received a script from Sheets which the filmmakers had copied in making *The Road to Glory*.

In his opening statement McCormick conceded that as was always the case in a plagiarism action, he could not present direct eyewitness testimony that a person or persons employed or engaged by Fox had been seen in the act of copying Sheets' scenario. However, he assured Judge Morris, he would present convincing and irrefutable evidence that in January of 1935, Sheets had typed out a motion picture scenario which he had entitled "The Road to Glory"; that Sheets had mailed this scenario from the United States Post Office in Jackson, Tennessee, to Twentieth Century Fox Film Corporation in Hollywood, California; that Fox had received Sheets' scenario; that one or more employees of Fox had read it; and that Fox had returned Sheets' scenario to him, ostensibly rejecting it.

Together with the facts regarding Sheets' composition of his play "Jeanne," which turned into "The Road to Glory," this would be the first phase of the plaintiff's proof, McCormick told Judge Morris, and by presenting it he would prove by a preponderance of the evidence—in point of fact, he said, by a totality of the evidence—that before Fox's filmmakers had ever given a scintilla of thought or consideration to the creation of the script from which they filmed *The Road to Glory*, Fox had **access** to Sheets' scenario bearing that very title.

The second phase of the plaintiff's proof, McCormick said, would consist of a detailed comparison of Sheets' scenario with the shooting script of the film, whereby Judge Morris would readily see the virtual identity of large portions of the two scripts. Fox had of course made certain changes such as the names of the principal characters, but so much of the dialogue and so many of the acting directions were exactly the same in the two scripts that Judge Morris would unquestionably find that Sheets had proven **similarity**.

Then, said McCormick, if His Honor pleased, with irrefutable proof of **access** and with **similarity** approaching identity in vast sections of the two scripts, the court would apply the law to the facts and find Fox guilty of plagiarism, after which the court would decide as to the monetary damages and other relief to be awarded to the plaintiff, Private Sheets.

McCormick sat down, Judge Morris nodded toward the defense table, and Dad rose from his chair. If it pleases the court, he said, the defense will prove that Private Sheets appears in court today to perpetrate an egregious fraud upon the defendant and the court. So saying, Dad sat down.

McCormick asked the Clerk to call his first witness. Sheets approached the Clerk, raised his right hand, put his left hand on the Bible, swore to tell the truth, the whole truth, and nothing but the truth, and sat down in the chair that constituted the witness stand. He gave his name as Robert H. Sheets, his age as 23, and his occupation as soldier in the United States Army, and in response to McCormick's questions he laid out his case as it had been described in his Bill of Complaint. McCormick concluded his direct examination of Sheets late that afternoon; turning to Dad, he said, "Your witness, Counselor," but Judge Morris adjourned Court before Dad could commence his cross-examination of Sheets.

Dad began his cross-examination of Sheets the following morning, November 10; he finished it on November 16. Midstream, McCormick wrote Pigford that Sheets had done well on direct examination, but that Wolf had gotten him so mixed up on cross-examination that Sheets had become confused about the different wordings of his handwritten manuscript, his typewritten scenario, and his script for his play "Jeanne" which had become "The Road to Glory" at Jackson High School and at Bells.

The fact was that McCormick, through no fault of his own, was the one who had become confused. Sheets had to thread his way through the minefield created by the identity of language in his manuscript with Bechdolt's invented language in Silver Screen, language which Sheets had massaged out of identity into similarity in the typescript. He knew exactly what he was doing, and he did it as well as it could be done. Dad had accused him of fraud in defendant's opening statement, and the handwritten manuscript, replete with deletions, insertions, and an occasional erasure, fit rather too nicely into the scheme Dad postulated. So Sheets sat on the witness stand and invented a double submission; he "suddenly" remembered what he had forgotten when he had given his deposition, which was that at the same time he sent his typewritten scenario to Fox, he had sent his handwritten scenario to Universal Scenario Company, and he could prove it. How, Dad asked? He produced correspondence dated from November 1934 through February 1935 which he had received from Universal Scenario, most of which referenced a manuscript entitled "Jeanne" but including a printed form bearing the title, in capital letters, THE ROAD TO GLORY. At Dad's request, the Clerk made a photostat of this exhibit and gave it to Dad.

On Tuesday, November 14, Judge Morris convened Court at the Fox Film Exchange rather than in the courtroom, and the day was devoted to going to the movies. After a complete screening, both sets of lawyers were permitted to have the projectionist rerun such parts as they selected. *The Evening Star* ran a large photograph of the judge viewing the film on its front page, and a photograph of everyone present at the screening on the continuation page.

Sheets left the witness stand on November 16. That night he reported to Albert Stone in Jackson in these words:

Just a few lines to tell you about yesterday's testimony. I left the stand about noon. We introduced the typewriter, and it was identified as being the machine used. This bit of evidence was unexpected and it hit them like an explosion of a bomb.

But the bomb blew up in Bob Sheets' face.

McCormick had followed the typewriter as it had traveled with the Miller Brothers from Lambuth College to Arkansas State University, and then into the hands of an acquaintance of theirs who continued to own it and readily loaned it back to them, and thus to McCormick, for use in the trial. McCormick well knew the impact of demonstrative evidence in a trial, and leapt at the opportunity to introduce into evidence *the very typewriter on which Sheets had typed his scenario.*

Before leaving the courtroom that day, Dad examined the typewriter and made careful note of the serial number engraved into a small metal plate affixed to the rear of the assembly. Returning to their office, he and Uncle Fulton telephoned George Wasson, Fox's in-house attorney, briefed him on the course of the trial to that point, and told him that they wanted Fox to permit them to make a substantial investment in private detectives. Wasson told them to go right ahead; on orders from Schenck and Zanuck, the defense budget was unlimited.

Dad then telephoned the Pinkerton Detective Agency in New York, spoke with the general manager, and explained his representation of Fox and what he wanted Pinkerton to do. An Underwood Model No. 5 is not much to go on, the manager said; do you by any chance have the serial number? Dad gave him the serial number and agreed on Fox's behalf to pay Pinkerton for expedited service, and Pinkerton was off and running.

McCormick paraded his witnesses on and off the witness stand until November 27. The Miller brothers gave their clear and convincing testimony concerning their faithful old typewriter, sitting before them among the exhibits, and McCormick buttressed their testimony by bringing their parents to Washington from Dexter, Missouri, to confirm that Mr. Miller had given his sons the typewriter in September of 1934 to take with them to college in Jackson, Tennessee. On cross-examination Mr. Miller, who owned the C. C. Miller Motor Company in Dexter, Missouri, testified that he had not bought the typewriter at a store of any kind, but had taken the typewriter in on trade for an old car because he wanted it for the boys. Numerous Jacksonians testified as to their roles in, or their viewing of, Sheets' play at Jackson High School. Dad cross-examined each Jackson witness with vigor, occasionally catching one up in a contradiction with his or her earlier deposition testimony, but Sheets' basic story remained intact, as Dad knew it would. Finally, McCormick announced that the plaintiff rested.

Dad decided that he had to put the screenwriting facts before the Court as the first order of business; Judge Morris made it clear that his priority was to hear the Fox testimony that would answer the question, Who wrote the script of *The Road to Glory?* Fully aware that the testimony of the production team was irremediably sloppy at best, Dad decided to present the testimony of Zanuck, Johnson, Hawks, and Avery, and various secretaries, stenographers, and flunkies, by having their deposition testimony read from the witness stand by an otherwise uninvolved reader. This was allowable under the Federal Rules due to the distance of these persons from the courthouse, so McCormick's objections—he could hardly wait to sink his teeth into these witnesses, all of whom he had roughed up substantially at their depositions—were overruled by the judge. Dad knew that as a matter of trial strategy, he would have to produce at least several live witnesses to testify as to the creation of the script; because they had been given screen credit as the writers, and because of their prominence, he called first William Faulkner and then Joel Sayre to the witness stand.

It was monumentally difficult to get William Faulkner to Washington to testify, not because Faulkner was unwilling to help—he and Dad had become fast friends in the course of pretrial preparation and McCormick's deposing of Faulkner—but because of Faulkner's well-known problem. The problem was alcohol. Dad decided to approach the problem by collaboration with Faulkner's wife. He and Mrs. Faulkner made an arrangement that Dad would telephone Mrs. Faulkner in Oxford, Mississippi, two weeks before the day that he wanted to put Faulkner on the witness stand. Mrs. Faulkner agreed that once she received Dad's telephone call, she would interdict any more liquor coming into the Faulkner home and would launch a search in order to appropriate and destroy such liquor already on the premises as she could find. However, she warned Dad, she and Faulkner had been through this procedure before, with mixed results. "Bill," she told Dad, "hides his liquor most imaginatively, Mr. Wolf, so I cannot promise you that I can deliver him to you. If he is still drinking at the time you send for him, he won't come, and I won't be able to make him."

Dad got a bottles-located-and-destroyed report from Mrs. Faulkner every other day for the following two weeks. The situation was nip and tuck, Mrs. Faulkner reported, but on the appointed evening Dad and Uncle Fulton went to the airport and met a haggard but sober William Faulkner who had come to Washington to do his duty. *The Evening Star* ran a photograph of noted author William Faulkner being met at the airport by his attorneys. I have the clipping; Faulkner looks terrible.

Faulkner's testimony was no worse than it had been on deposition. The judge being honored to have such a famous personage in his courtroom, Dad asked Faulkner a few questions about his contribution to the script of *The Road to Glory*, and while the judge nodded affirmatively Faulkner described his vital contribution. Then Dad turned him over to McCormick's untender mercies, and

McCormick had a predictable field day. McCormick handed Faulkner a copy of the shooting script, complete with the Ferrises' blue pages; when it came to identifying *words on paper*, Faulkner was unable to identify a single sentence that was his very own creation. The judge's awe turned to exasperation, and Dad made no attempt to resurrect Faulkner on redirect examination. The judge excused Faulkner with markedly less enthusiasm than he had shown upon seeing him take the witness stand. Faulkner wandered out of the courtroom and out of the lawsuit, but before he left Washington, he went to a bookstore, bought a copy of his famous novel "Sanctuary," inscribed it "To Bill Wolf, After the Barrage Lifted," and left it at Dad's office. Boxed, it hangs on our reception room wall today.

Joel Sayre's experience on the witness stand has been better put in a letter McCormick wrote to Pigford than I could ever describe it. Here is what McCormick wrote:

Sayre commenced work on this picture in the late fall of 1935 and remained at the studio on this picture until January 26, 1936, when the shooting script was completed. After he and Faulkner completed the script of December 31, 1935, two additional scripts were turned out, one dated January 14, 1936, and one dated January 26, 1936. Sayre was asked on direct examination [i.e., by Dad] to state the manner in which these two latter scripts were written. He testified for a day and a half in response to this and similar questions on direct examination. After a half day of cross examination [by McCormick], it appeared that he had given credit to someone else for all of those portions of the script in which we were interested, and that he himself claimed only three lines of dialogue in one scene.

I then asked him why he had received screen credit as being one of the authors of the play. He fainted.

Two days later he returned to the stand and stated that he had read his testimony, particularly his cross examination, and that he wanted to correct his testimony, stating that it appeared from the testimony as though he had done nothing except card tricks during the month of January, 1936, but actually he had contributed a great deal to the two scripts which were completed in January. I then asked him how he was feeling and if he had fully recovered from his indisposition earlier in the week. He replied that he had fully recovered, was feeling fine, and that the doctor advised there was nothing wrong with him.

I then handed him the script of January 14, 1936, and asked him to commence at the front and point out each line, each situation and each scene to which he had contributed.

He again fainted without answering the question.

Two weeks later, at the conclusion of the evidence Sayre again returned to the witness stand. I decided on the record not to cross examine him further, hoping that the other side would not spend any time on redirect because I felt that Sayre was obviously a dangerous witness to the defendant. However, when Sayre took the stand and I announced that I had no further questions, Wolf related to Sayre, by way of refreshing his recollection, that he had twice fainted when asked to point out in detail the contributions which he had made to the two scripts of January, 1936. Wolf then asked him how he was feeling and got into the record the fact that Sayre had spent two and one-half hours the evening before discussing his testimony with Wolf and particularly discussing the answer to that very question. Wolf then asked him to point out in those two scripts the contributions which he had made to them.

Sayre again fainted without answering the question, and when the record finally closed, those questions were still unanswered by Sayre.

Dad had an exquisite sense of trial timing. His case had hit rock bottom; Faulkner and Sayre had been testimonial disasters without mitigation, as he knew (but hoped otherwise) that they would be. So it was time for the defense to adhere to the ancient maxim and launch its offensive against Sheets.

Dad's offensive had three prongs. Sheets had offered into evidence his "Application" to Universal Scenario Company which had indisputably been sent in by him over the period December 1934

- February 1935. This document showed the title of his submission to be THE ROAD TO GLORY. Sheets had testified that he had not typed the "Application" on the Miller brothers' Underwood Model No. 5, but on a Woodstock typewriter belonging to one Zelma Ernst, and Zelma had brought her typewriter to Washington and testified to the same effect with her typewriter in hand. No argument so far. But the background behind the words THE ROAD TO GLORY bore a sizable smudge which led to what turned out to be a non-battle of typewriter experts. Both experts testified that THE ROAD TO GLORY had been typed over an erasure. Neither expert could testify as to the word or words that had been erased, but nonetheless Dad had scored an important point by placing in the mind of the judge the probability that the word that had been erased was JEANNE, because all of the other correspondence Sheets had had with Universal Scenario and introduced into evidence related to JEANNE. Had Sheets overplayed his hand?

The second prong of the defense's offense consisted of an exhaustive comparison of Sheets' handwritten manuscript and his typewritten manuscript with Jack Bechdolt's reproduction—and romantic expansion—of the shooting script in Silver Screen. Dad called Jack Bechdolt as his next witness.

Bechdolt testified that his editor at Silver Screen magazine had handed him the shooting script of *The Road to Glory* in April of 1936. He read the script and saw the challenge. He had no knowledge of Zanuck's purchase of the war photography from Pathé-Natan, but being very familiar with Hawks' work, he knew that Hawks' battle footage would be first-rate. His challenge was to take the script of a film replete with scenes of war and make it appeal to a largely female reading public.

He did this by incorporating large sections of dialogue from scenes in which the female character, Monique, expresses her love for Lieutenant Delsage and her pity for the blinded commanding officer, Captain Marache. Bechdolt testified that his task included not only linking the extracted passages together to give the reader a sense of plot, but to create the impression that there was considerably more romance in the film than was actually the case.

Bechdolt pointed out two examples of what he termed his "expansion" of the script. One was his addition of a line he gave to Monique reading "Goodbye! Goodbye Paul * * * God guard you and bring you back safe from the trenches." The other was the final sentence of his article, made up by him out of whole cloth: "She was the light that went before, leading his weary feet along the road to glory."

This testimony was of enormous significance. These passages appeared nowhere in any Fox script or in the film, but they appeared in Silver Screen magazine and in both Sheets' handwritten scenario and his typewritten scenario. In the handwritten scenario, Sheets had the mother of a soldier named Paul say "Goodbye! Goodbye Paul * * * God guard you and bring you back ~~to me~~ from the trenches," and he carried this line forward in his typescript to read "Goodbye! Goodbye Paul * * * God guard you and bring you back safe from the trenches." And Sheets had ended his handwritten scenario with the lines "Jeanne ~~was~~ is the light that ~~led * * *~~ ~~went~~ goes before, leading his feet along the road to glory," carrying these lines forward in his typescript to read "Jeanne is the light that goes before, leading his weary feet along the road to glory."

This testimony would have sent many a plagiarist slinking from the courtroom, but not Bob Sheets. He remounted the witness stand on rebuttal and endeavored to explain away this damning testimony by suddenly, and at that late hour in the trial, recalling that shortly before he typed the scenario he had introduced into evidence at the beginning of the trial as the scenario he had mailed to Fox, he had prepared an earlier scenario and sent it to the Universal Scenario Company! This scenario, he explained brightly to the judge, must have found its way to Fox, and Fox must have sent it to Mr. Bechdolt at Silver Screen!

After giving this testimony, Sheets sat back in the witness chair bathed in self-satisfaction. One look at Judge Morris and

McCormick was unable to share any part of Sheets' satisfaction. For Dad, it was typewriter time.

Sheets had unequivocally identified the typewriter in the courtroom as the typewriter on which he had written his scenario in December of 1934 and January of 1935, but Dad did not want to leave him an "out" whereby he could change his story, so his first typewriter witness was a typewriter identification expert who had examined and tested the machine, compared its product with Sheets' scenario, and testified from comparison blowups he had made that there could be no doubt that the scenario had been typed on that machine. McCormick, whose case hinged on that very fact, did not cross-examine. In rebuttal, he called his own typewriter expert to the witness stand to reinforce this testimony.

Dad then called the Pinkerton man to the stand. He testified that, utilizing the serial number on the Underwood Model No. 5 typewriter sitting among the trial exhibits, he had traced its provenance from its manufacture by the Underwood Typewriter Company to its sale by a Chicago office supply company to an owner who had traded it in on a newer model at a Montgomery Ward store in Peoria, Illinois. Montgomery Ward's records revealed that it had rebuilt the typewriter and sold it through its catalogue to a Reverend Frank Stickney of Grandin, Missouri, in 1932.

Dad's next witness was the Reverend Frank Stickney. He confirmed that he had purchased the typewriter from Montgomery Ward in October or November of 1932. He testified that he had bought it for his daughter, who kept it for several years and then, shortly before Christmas of 1934, gave it to her brother, his son Virgil.

Then Virgil Stickney took the stand. He testified that just after Christmas, some time early in January of 1935, he and his wife Ruth took the typewriter to the home of his wife's grandfather, Reverend F. M. Fowler, in Dexter, Missouri, where it remained until that summer or fall. He was not sure of the date or even the month, but he was sure of the year, because at some time between August and November of 1935 he went to Reverend Fowler's home, retrieved the typewriter, took it to the C. C. Miller Motor Company in Dexter and traded it to Mr. Miller for an old car, a 1923 Buick.

Dad asked him, "Why was Mr. Miller willing to trade you a car for the typewriter?"

"Because," he answered, "the old car was in very bad condition and needed a lot of work, which I knew how to do, and Mr. Miller said he needed the typewriter for his two sons who were off at some college."

Dad then introduced into evidence the sworn certificate of the Secretary of State of the State of Missouri attesting to the fact that on October 22, 1935, registration of the 1923 Buick in question had been transferred from one R. H. Seeburger of Dexter, Missouri, to Ruth Stickney of Dexter, Missouri.

Dad's next witness was Richard H. Seeburger. He testified that he had purchased a brand new 1935 Plymouth automobile from the C. C. Miller Motor Company of Dexter, Missouri, in July of 1935, trading in his old 1923 Buick in partial payment for his new car.

Then Dad pinned down the trade-in date as not possibly being before the month of March, 1935, by calling a Plymouth dealer to the witness stand. This witness testified that Plymouth introduced its 1935 models in December of 1934, and that the serial number of Mr. Seeburger's purchase identified it as a vehicle which could not have reached the dealership any earlier than March of 1935.

Dad's closing argument tied together all of the typewriter evidence which had been gathered by the Pinkerton Agency and presented through live and unimpeachable witnesses. The Miller brothers and their parents were simply wrong in testifying that Mr. Miller had given his sons the Underwood Model No. 5 in the Fall of 1934, as conclusively proven by the testimony that this typewriter had not come into the possession of Mr. Miller until the Fall of 1935.

Thus, Dad argued convincingly, Sheets was absolutely correct

in testifying that he typed his scenario on the Miller boys' typewriter; Sheets was sure of this, the expert witnesses for both plaintiff and defendant confirmed it, and on behalf of Fox, Dad enthu-
siastically agreed. But Sheets' testimony that he typed his scenario
on this typewriter in December of 1934 and January of 1935 was
a brazen, bold-faced lie—arrant perjury, Dad characterized it—
because in December of 1934 and January of 1935, the typewriter was in Missouri, not in Tennessee. But, Dad continued,
this typewriter did make its way to Tennessee in the Fall of 1935.
It was still there, in the Miller brothers' dormitory room at Lambuth
College in Jackson, when the July issue of Silver Screen magazine
hit the newsstands and beauty parlors and libraries of America on
June 5, 1936, and it remained there just long enough for Mr.
Sheets to perpetrate his egregious fraud on Fox and on the Court.

  To his credit, McCormick made a very strong closing argument which focussed on the patent inability of the Fox witnesses
to identify who wrote what parts of the shooting script. After making mincemeat out of the live testimony of Faulkner and Sayre,
and pointing out the gross inconsistencies in the deposition testimony of Zanuck, Johnson, Avery, Hawks, and the Ferrises as each
one endeavored first to avoid and then to confront McCormick's
simple question, "What lines did you, sir, write?" McCormick gave
the judge *his* scenario of the scripting of *The Road to Glory.* By
January of 1936, Darryl Zanuck and Nunnally Johnson had wasted
a great deal of studio money on Stephen Avery, then Joel Sayre,
then of all people William Faulkner, as famous for his drinking as
he was for his writing. Hawks was already on the payroll, drawing
a vast salary, and he had cast three of Hollywood's most expensive
stars whose unimaginable salaries were to start, ready or not, on
February 1. But Zanuck had no script; the writers' notes, which
McCormick had obtained in the course of these men's depositions, made it plain, McCormick argued, that what Zanuck then
had was his precious war footage and a mess. Suddenly—*suddenly*,
argued McCormick—Zanuck had a filmable script. Where did it
come from? There could have only been a single source: Robert H.

Sheets! McCormick could not be held to account for every peregrination of Sheets' scenario in Hollywood, but McCormick was confident that Zanuck knew, and Johnson knew, and if the writers had stopped drinking and hunting and fishing and quarreling long enough to pay attention, they knew, too, that from a source completely unknown to any of them, Zanuck had suddenly and mysteriously converted their foolish notions and jottings into a mature and sophisticated film script, virtually ready for the camera.

McCormick then did his level best to discredit the Tale of the Typewriter. Mr. Wolf, he told the Court, wishes you to disregard the testimony of the Miller brothers and numerous Jacksonians, none of whom has the slightest financial interest in this case, but to credit the testimony of a family of Missouri farm folk claiming to remember when they passed an old typewriter from hand to hand. I shall be charitable, he said, and characterize their testimony as merely unreliable, while Mr. Wolf wants the Court to believe that there lives not a single honest man or woman in the town of Jackson, Tennessee. Etc., etc.

The trial concluded in early February of 1940. Judge Morris took the case under advisement, announcing that he intended to review all of the evidence, read every deposition, and give the matter his most careful consideration before rendering his verdict.

On April 26, 1940, McCormick wrote to Pigford to tell him he had been informed by friendly clerks at the United States Courthouse that Judge Morris was hard at work writing his opinion. In this letter, McCormick afforded Pigford a concise view of the issues. He wrote:

The present situation may be concretely summed up in this fashion. There is no evidence to contradict the testimony of our corroborating witnesses. If the Court believes the testimony of these witnesses, then it must find that our manuscript was in existence in January of 1935, or many months prior to the time the defendant claims it commenced work on the production of the script. If the Court also believes the testimony of Sheets and his mother that a copy of the manuscript was forwarded to the defendant, then I feel there will be a finding in favor of the plaintiff. If either of these factors are decided against us, then we must lose the case. The Court could, but I hope it will not, ignore these two major factors and make an affirmative decision upholding one of the defenses of the defendant. This would inferentially rule against us on one of the two factors first mentioned.

Judge Morris rendered his twenty-six page opinion on June 4, 1940. He meticulously detailed the moviemaking process and thoroughly detailed what he considered to be the probative evidence. He found plagiarism, of course, but it was *by* Sheets, not *of* Sheets. McCormick sent to the courthouse for a copy of the opinion and immediately wrote to Pigford. This is what he wrote:

Dear Mr. Pigford:

"The Moving Finger writes; and having writ
Moves on; nor all your Piety nor Wit
Shall lure it back to cancel half a Line,
Nor all your Tears wash out a Word of it."

The court finds that Sheets copied from the
Silver Screen some time during the month of
June, 1936; that he used the Miller boys'
typewriter during that month to make his
typewritten copy; that our witnesses did not
see a copy of his manuscript in January
of 1935 but did see a copy of the Legion
play by the same name at that time; that
Sheets never submitted a copy of his
manuscript to the 20th Century people; and
that the bill of complaint must be dismissed
at the cost of the plaintiff.

Thus ended *Sheets v. Twentieth Century Fox Film Corporation,* but that was not the end of the matter. Judge Morris referred it to the Department of Justice for investigation as to whether perjury had been committed in his court, and for many months thereafter agents of the Federal Bureau of Investigation pored over the transcript of the trial and interviewed Sheets' witnesses in Jackson, Tennessee, and in Jefferson City, Missouri. The probability is that the Imperial Japanese Fleet, specifically its Air Arm, kept Private Sheets in the Army and out of jail; from and after December 7, 1941, the FBI had more important things to do than pursue the Sheets Case.

From and after December 7, 1941, so did Dad; although over draft age, he enlisted in the Army not long after Pearl Harbor was bombed, shedding his Lieutenant Colonelcy and his khaki uniform to return to the practice of law in November, 1945. However, at some time after June 4, 1940, he too turned his hand to poesy, not Omar the Tentmaker's, but his very own. Although certain of the references remain mysterious, one cannot help but get the general idea:

"The Road to Glory from A to Z"
(How to reduce a 26-page opinion to 26 lines)

A is for Authorship, matter of doubt;
B is the Black Book, which helped us find out.
C stands for romantic music by "Choppin:;
D for De Shazo who hopped - and kept hoppin'.
E's for Exhibit B, also Elite;
F is Bill Faulkner (to read, quite a feat).
G - or 5 G's - to the Gal-friend for lying;
H for Heart Cases. (Can't hate him for trying!)
I's International Exchange, far away;
J is for Jackson, Tenn. - also Jeanné.
K's for Kay Kyser, and Ed Kilroe's hooey;
L's Lambuth, Laundry, and Legion Play (phooey!).
M not McCormick, but March and his wimmin;
N is for Nunn'ly, deposing while swimmin'.

O for that massive luck-wisher called "Ox";
P for the Pinkertons, peeping for Fox.
Q stands for Questions that fathomed the tale;
R's Robert, Raleigh, and Registered Mail.
S means "suggestion" and Silver Screen Sniping
T for Tux-photos - and Terrible Typing.
U's Universal, "defunct gyp concern";
V is for Virgil, who spoke out of turn.
W's Woodstock, and Wertheim (for Si!)
X is the expert who didn't know Pi.
Y's Young Collegians who footballed all day
and Z's Darryl Zanuck who wrote the damn play.

"OBITER DICTA"

Lawyer Joke I: Two young hotshot associates in a large firm share a secretary—day and night. The secretary becomes pregnant. When she reaches term, one of the associates happens to be in London on firm business. The other associate sends him a fax: "Marge had twins. Mine died."

Lawyer Joke II: Flushed with victory after a long, tough trial, the lawyer faxes his out-of-town client "JUSTICE HAS TRIUMPHED!" The client faxes back "APPEAL IMMEDIATELY!"

Obsession: There was a wonderful old man who had practiced tax law brilliantly and successfully for twenty years when an inventor came into his office bearing a patent issued to him by the United States Patent Office for the metallic shielding of dynamos, magnetos, and other sorts of engines. It was this invention, the inventor explained, which had made possible the transmission of voice by radio to and from ground stations and aircraft and from plane to plane; without it, the only radio communication possible was by Morse or similar code.

The old man, wearying of a life spent with the Internal Revenue Code as his constant professional companion, was intrigued. He investigated the inventor and the patent; both checked out. He wrote letters of demand to the United States Government, all of the manufacturers of aircraft radio equipment, and all of the major airlines, demanding that royalties be paid to the inventor. His demands were refused.

The inventor told the old man that he was wanted to pursue the matter in the courts, but that he had very little money. The old man responded in several ways: He located a retired Federal judge who was willing to institute litigation against all putative infringers, including the Government, on a contingent fee basis, and he agreed to finance the ancillary costs of what would be expensive litigation in return for a share in the patent. The inventor was delighted with the arrangement; gradually, as expenses mounted, the old man came to own 55% of the inventor's patent.

Lawsuits were duly filed against the radio manufacturers and the airlines in various Federal courts, and against the Government in the United States Court of Claims. By agreement, the suits against the manufacturers and the airlines were stayed pending the outcome of the suit against the Government. The lawsuit in the Court of Claims was stayed throughout World War II, most of the necessary witnesses being otherwise occupied.

When World War II ended, the legal proceedings were resumed in the Court of Claims. Extensive testimony was taken throughout the United States, argument was had before the Court, and the Court reserved judgment until it had reviewed all of the transcripts and exhibits.

The delays and the expenses took their toll on the old man. He let his tax law practice founder and ultimately disappear, and spent his days and night writing memoranda to the trial lawyer, the retired judge. All of his money spent on the case and the inventor, the old man drove away his friends and haunted his relatives with demands that they purchase percentages of the patent from him, as he had done with the inventor, so that he could buy groceries, pay his rent, and continue to support the inventor and the lawsuit; neither friends nor relatives had the slightest faith in the lawsuit, but two of his in-laws paid his rent, bought his groceries, provided a maid when his beloved wife became very ill and completely bedridden, and gave him a little pocket money which he of course applied to the lawsuit.

Knowing that he had become an object of derision within the circle of his friends and family, he became bitter. His bitterness manifested itself first in uncharacteristic irascibility, then in articulated rage. Totally obsessed with the lawsuit and pouring out suggestions to the retired judge and venom to his supporting relatives, he took sick and died. The news of his death was kept from his adoring wife for several days; finally disclosed, it sent her to her death within two weeks.

Three months after the old man's death the Court of Claims handed down its decision. The Court held that the patent had been infringed by the shielding on each and every one of the eighty-odd magnetos and engines on each and every B-17 bomber flown by the United States Army Air Corps during World War II, and by each and every lesser number of same on every other military air-craft owned and flown by the United States Government. The world press quickly got copies of the Court's holding, and publi-cized it around the globe; Fortune magazine published its esti-mate of the claimants' damages as in the neighborhood of fifty million dollars; the children of the old man, who at his death owned 55% of the patent, were identified as the principal benefi-ciaries of the lawsuit.

The old man's middle-aged son parlayed the newspaper and magazine reports into a large bank loan which enabled him to quit his long-time job as a store manager and go into business for him-self; the old man's daughter remained skeptical of the ultimate outcome.

Exactly one year after the decision was issued, the Govern-ment moved to reopen the trial on the basis of newly-discovered evidence. The Court granted this motion, and a further hearing was held. The Government called a new witness, an Australian who had with him a pamphlet he had located in a library in New South Wales. The pamphlet, written by Guglielmo Marconi him-self and dated four years earlier than the patent, dealt with the possibility of shielding and contained an outline sketch which ar-guably but remotely resembled the key drawing in the patent.

The Court of Claims held that the Marconi sketch constituted "prior art" and thus vitiated the inventor's patent, and entered judg-ment for the Government. The civil suits were thereby deemed mere nuisances and settled for a pittance by the old man's executor. The old man's son was crushed by the reversal; his business venture went into bankruptcy, and his life into chaos. Only the old man's daughter was unaffected; she had never for one minute believed in the patent or the lawsuit, or that she was a millionairess. She had only believed that her father, who had been very dear to her, had driven himself mad and then into his grave in pursuit of a chimera.

Mother Love I: Fran telephoned my office to make an appointment "on a desperate matter of child custody." She came to my office in highest upset; her husband had walked out on her and their two little children, and was now, through counsel, demanding the right to have the children with him every other weekend.

"I wish to retain you to make sure that that bastard *never sees my children again*," was how she put my mission.

I explained to Fran that such an outcome was unlikely, but that I would commence negotiations with her husband's lawyer, looking for financial contribution and a reasonable visitation schedule respecting the children; perhaps I could confine her husband's visits to her home and one day a month.

"Nothing more," she said, "or I'll move away and take the children to where he'll never find us."

I opened negotiations, which quickly bogged down on the subject of money; a month went by and Fran's husband's lawyer had not yet taken up the subject of child custody and visitation. I reported to Fran; she said, "The rotten rat hasn't even telephoned his children."

Two weeks later Fran came to my office to review where negotiations stood; her husband still had not telephoned the children, nor had he made any effort to see them. "I thought you were going to arrange for a monthly visitation for the children," she said. "He hasn't even called. Tell his lawyer that he can come to see them next Saturday morning."

I duly telephoned her husband's lawyer with this information. The lawyer said she would convey the message to her client and get back to me. She called back about a week later to say that the visitation schedule I had proposed was acceptable to her client.

I called Fran. She said, "I want you to know that I telephoned that piece of you-know-what and asked him when he was coming to see *his* children, and he hung up on me!"

I said, "Well, there is good news. I think I have the monetary matters settled to your satisfaction, and he has agreed to our visitation schedule. I should have an Agreement ready for signature in a couple of days."

"Stop working," Fran ordered. "I don't care what the Agreement says. I won't sign....unless...."

"Unless what?" I demanded.

"Unless that rotten, negligent, uncaring son-of-a-bitch *takes* the children!"

"For an entire weekend?" I asked in confusion.

"*Permanently*," Fran replied. "I mean, for good!"

"What happened, Fran?" I asked gently.

"They are driving me nuts," she replied just as gently, "and I'm sick and tired of them. But I would like *some* visitation rights; maybe one day a month, at his place...."

Mother Love II: She was tall and slender, dressed à la Peck & Peck, an attractive woman in her mid-thirties with sun-streaked brown hair and early signs of lines in her face. I doubted that a sense of humor would be discernible, even in good times.

She appeared to be certain that no one in the world, including me, had the ability to comprehend her utterly unique problem, but she was determined to try to communicate it to me. She addressed me in the manner in which you address a child when you are trying to explain something that you know the child will not completely understand.

Oh, well. I listened patiently, and tried to encourage her by looking as if I had never heard such a story before.

She had been married for twelve years to a man who was thoroughly decent. They had three perfectly spaced children, aged nine, six, and three. Her husband was a highly regarded and eminently successful partner in a large national firm of certified public accountants. She and he had started married life in a small apartment on Connecticut Avenue. They had moved twice, first into a modest rambler in American University Park and then, three years ago, into a large Tudor-style home in Spring Valley, one of Washington's most elegant neighborhoods. The two older children were in private school.

She had been wretchedly unhappy for the last two years; probably much longer than that without knowing it. She had found that getting to the root of what was making her miserable was very difficult, but now she knew both what was troubling her and the solution.

She had decided to get a divorce. No, she had not told her husband of her decision, because she thought that she should get legal advice before doing that, but her decision had been made. How was she to go about it?

I told her that it was essential that I know the *reason* for her decision before I could give her more than superficial counsel.

"My husband," she said, "is a fine man and a wonderful father—I want him to see the children as often as he wishes—but I cannot spend the rest of my life with him."

I persisted in needing to know the *reason*.

"He works terribly hard, year 'round, not just at tax time, although at tax time, I barely see him from the first of February until the fifteenth of April, and when we go to the beach in the Summer, he stays for a few days and then leaves us there until it's time to return home. For a lot of years I thought that this was the way it should be—after all, he is an excellent provider—until I finally realized that this was by his choice. So far as he is concerned, I have become a stick of furniture."

I dug deeper.

"Oh, he never forgets to give me a nice gift on my birthday and at Christmas—and on our anniversary, too—and if the subject comes up, he tells me that he loves me, but he rarely reaches for me...."

She hesitated; I sat, stonefaced.

"....at night—maybe once a month, at tax time."

She sat back; she had told me enough to make me see the unique situation she was in. I remained silent.

"I can't stand it. When we get together with friends, they are always laughing together, radiating warmth. I....I can't do that."

"How does your husband act among friends?" I asked.

"He's warm and witty with everybody."

"With you?" I asked gently.

"He tries to be," she answered, "but it doesn't work with me."

She repeated her metaphor. "I know that I'm just a stick of furniture to him."

I bled for the poor guy.

"Will you take my case?" she asked.

"No," I said, "because you left too much out of your story."

As I knew it would, her hostility erupted instantly.

"You need the sexual details, eh?" she snarled.

"No, but you left out the dog. It's probably a golden retriever."

This took her aback. Finally she said, "Yes, we have a dog, and yes, it's a golden retriever."

"And you left out the station wagon," I continued.

She got up from her chair. From between clenched teeth came, "We have a station wagon. *What else did I leave out?*"

"The man on the beach."

She turned ashen.

"You remember," I continued. "The man you met on the beach last Summer. The man who made you feel like a woman again." If she had been a little less upset, she might have thrown something at me, or at least knocked over a piece of furniture, but as it was, she just ran out of my room and out of the office.

I decided not to bill her for my time.